The Flaw

ANTONIS SAMARAKIS

The Flaw

Translated by
Simon Darragh

AI♀RA

Original title: *Το Λάθος*

ISBN: 978-618-5048-77-8

AIORA PRESS
11 Mavromichali St.
Athens 10679 - Greece
tel: +30 210 3839000
www.aiorabooks.com

For Elenitsa

NO, I DIDN'T HEAR WHAT HE SAID TO ME. Just then an enormous refrigerator lorry was passing us. Fruit, I think; I'm not sure. Well, first of all, the lorry was raising a cloud of dust, and second, it made such a noise it was impossible to hear.

'What did you say?' I asked him, 'I could see you were saying something, but what with the commotion of that lorry I didn't catch a word.'

The Manager gave me a sidelong look as if it were too much effort to say it again. Finally, he decided. 'I asked you what the hell you were up to with all this looking out the window.'

I didn't answer straight away; first, I jangled my keys. I usually have them in my hand, on a ring, and I play with them. Then I scratched my right ear—the right?— and announced, 'I'm enjoying nature!'

He went 'Ah!' as if he had a kidney stone, or a wasp had stung him, or he had seen a ghost or something.

And he looked at me with a grin. But what a grin! All camouflaged irony.

'Forgive me,' I said, 'It didn't occur to me that it might annoy you that I enjoy nature. I see it now in your expression. But tell me, doesn't nature move you? No? This idyllic scene, bracketed, as it were between, these dull grey industrial areas we're going through.'

He gave me a cold stare and said nothing. As for the half-ironic grin, one might think it was stuck there.

'Who do you think you are, not saying anything?' I went on. 'Does this panorama around us mean nothing to you? The little, low hills, as if moulded by a friendly hand; the tall, slim trees right and left, as if standing to attention for us. The little stream rolling on and on... the birds that cut the air and glide down to greet us. And the multi-coloured wildflowers—what a charming sight!—pouring out their intoxicating perfume.'

He went 'Oh!' as if he had a kidney stone or a wasp had stung him, etc., etc.

'You know what you are?' I hurled at him, 'Or rather, what you aren't? Well, you're not normal. I bet you're full of complexes.'

'You think I've got a complex?' he said, as if talking to himself.

'Of course! Take the present circumstances. Nature opens her arms wide to us, an orgy of colours and scents, and you couldn't care less. The enchanting landscape around us doesn't exist for you. The charming dolls-house cottages with their red roofs and green and yellow windows, the children singing and playing, surrounded by poultry, grunting piglets and various other farm animals...'

'Poultry, piglets... grunting piglets and various other farm animals,' he said, like a pupil repeating after his teacher.

'Come,' I tried to encourage him, 'Open your eyes, and take in the superb pale pink that gently colours the horizon. Open your heart, and—'

'Enough!' he interrupted, 'I'm guilty! Yes, I should have noticed the scenery, and been moved by it.'

And he tilted back his trilby, which had fallen down and was obstructing his view.

'At last!' I sighed, delighted by the change, 'Better late than...'

'Yes, over there on the right, at the farmhouse with the yellow windows and lots of balconies,' he said, pointing. 'First, no, second balcony on the right. I see a charming pink...'

'...rose?'

'Pair of knickers.'

'Shame on you!'

'Excuse me, why "shame on you"?' he protested. 'I saw them clearly, I tell you! Honestly! That chubby girl who reached up to clean the windows is wearing pink knickers!'

'Shame on you.'

'And lacy ones, too.'

There was no point continuing the conversation. My nerves were dancing as if under a pneumatic drill. To relieve them I leant out of the right window and spat. The wind brought my spit faithfully back, spraying my face. Into my right eye.

A silence intervened that lasted a quarter of an hour, maybe longer.

At some point I saw the Manager steer with his left hand only and search his pockets with the right. One after the other, continuously. What the hell was he looking for, for so long? No, I wasn't keen on this; it's no joke to drive with one hand on National Route 37 at 9.20 in the morning, the road choked up with traffic, and with the other hand searching your pockets. And what's more, with the speedometer at a steady 110 kilometres an hour.

Finally, from a jacket or waistcoat pocket—the latest style of waistcoat, yellow and black check, I liked it a lot—he brought out some tablets of chewing gum.

'There, I've found them!' he shouted excitedly. 'Me, whenever I'm going on a journey, I put some pieces of chewing gum in my pockets. Just the thing! They quench your thirst. It's just that I can never find them straight away. It often happens that I forget which pocket I put them in, and since I'm full of pockets, large and small, sometimes I have to make a thorough search.'

He took a piece for himself, started to chew it and, leaning to his right, gave two to the man sitting in the middle. 'One each,' he said.

'OK,' he said, taking the pieces, 'I've got a terrible thirst!'

He kept his and, leaning to his right, gave me the other one. No, I didn't have a fearful thirst, I didn't have any kind of thirst, but I took it; why not?

I wouldn't say we were very comfortable with the three of us in front, but nor that we were very cramped. Two and a half hours earlier, at seven, when we talked of setting off, the Manager had the idea that we should all three sit in front. 'It's better like that! One next to the other, we can chat, and we won't notice the journey.'

We agreed unanimously. Well, we got in, and at first we had to squeeze a bit. As for the suitcases, we put them on the back seat.

'You know what?' said the Manager, chewing his gum, 'We won't just be on time for the ferry, but a quarter of an hour or twenty minutes early. This car is a beauty!'

'Not just the car, but the driver, too!' our man said and winked at me.

'He's a beauty, too?'

'What I mean is, he's a fine driver.'

'Well, on that I agree. The Manager is a maestro at the wheel.'

'Tell me, why are you so interested in me?' asked the Manager with a smile. 'Are you two teasing me? Anyway, I'm happy to accept compliments!'

I was going to add something, but in the end didn't say anything. I was just then prevented by a pain in my stomach.

It was last Wednesday, a week ago today, that this mysterious pain first appeared. I was in the office, writing or phoning—yes, phoning—when it came on suddenly with no warning.

It wasn't exactly what you'd call 'pain'. It was as if someone prodded me, but hard, with a finger. It lasted a second, then it went away, and suddenly it came back again. Then it stopped completely.

But since then not a day has gone by without it. Three or four times a day, at various times and without warning. In the office, at home, on the street...

At thirty-five years old, this is the first problem I've had with my stomach. The strange thing is that my wife is more worried about it than I am. She moaned at me continually not to waste time, to go and get examined as quickly as possible, that's to say, at once. Not that I wasn't worried. But what with work at the office—and in recent days there'd been more than ever—where was the spare time for visits to doctors? The truth is there's another reason: I'm a ditherer by nature.

Anyway, I would have gone at the first opportunity. I had in mind a gastric specialist warmly recommended by a friend at work. Just to get the worry off my mind, nothing else. Nerves, it would be. Probably. Too much work at the office, too much worry, too much coffee, too many cigarettes.

'Crossroads ahead!' the Manager announced, as if he were saying, 'Hands up!'

'No, really?' I said. 'We've got to the crossroads already?'

'Yes, indeed!' the Manager continued, 'What did you expect? Eating up time at 110, distances become nothing. In ten minutes we'll be at the crossing with National Route 40. Then we leave 37 and get on to 40, and zip! Port and ferry!'

'Fine!' I said, 'So everything's going well so far.'

The Manager was quiet then, because as we approached the junction the traffic became a nightmare, and he had to have eyes in the back of his head.

'What's that scar under your ear?' I asked the man, 'It's the first time I've seen it; I'd never noticed it until now.'

'Oh, that's an old story,' he said, chewing the Manager's gum. 'Streptococcus'.

'Oh yes?'

'I was still a child, sixteen, and I got a streptococcus infection. Fifteen years ago! Anyway, the streptococcus got me there, at the base of the right ear. There was a huge swelling. They did an operation, quite a deep cut, to get the pus out and clean it. And the operation left that scar.'

'Actually, it doesn't show much. I mean, it shows, but you have to look hard. Anyway, you could go to a specialist to get rid of it; it's very simple.'

'I've thought of it.'

'So why didn't you decide to do it? Are you afraid?'

He laughed. 'I can't be bothered. But I'll get it done, now you mention it. Yes, when we get back from the capital I'll see to it.'

At the crossroads we ran into trouble. Something had happened, a crash—a bus and a lorry or another bus, it was hard to make it out, and anyway it didn't matter. All that mattered was that we had got caught up in a traffic jam. It was chaos, a mass of gridlocked cars.

'We're done for!' sighed the Manager as he braked. 'The way the jam gets longer and longer, we're well caught up in it. There's no need to philosophise: the ferry won't delay its departure for the sake of our lovely eyes. At 11.10, 11.10 exactly, it'll weigh anchor, no matter what happens.'

I got out of the car and went down into the fields. 'I'll be back at once,' I told them, 'I'll be done in two minutes.'

'Behind the fence!' the Manager shouted. 'Why are you looking at me? Go straight behind the fence, no-one will see you there, even with binoculars.'

'Oh, no,' I shouted back, 'I'm not going for what you think,' and I headed for a bank of wildflowers that I'd spotted. I quickly made a perfect bouquet. Some lovely little flowers whose name I don't know.

I arranged my flowers carefully below the windscreen. Not by myself. He helped me in the arrangement, he was eager to do it. As for the Manager, he threw us glances full of his familiar camouflaged irony.

'The Manager's chewing gum has gone and got stuck in my tooth,' the other chap complained. 'I've got a tooth, here on the right, the last but one in the upper jaw, and it's been bad for some time. If cold, let alone ice-cold, water gets on it, or bits of food, the pain drives me crazy.'

'What are you waiting for?' I said, 'Why don't you go and get a filling? It might need a crown. For now, accept this flower, for your help in arranging the bouquet. Put it in your buttonhole.'

He was excited, as if I'd given him I don't know what. He fitted the little flower—it was mauve—in his buttonhole, and even checked his reflection in the windscreen to see how it looked.

'Look at me,' he said proudly, 'the perfect dandy! A flower in my buttonhole—don't I look the part?'

Fortunately, the jam quickly cleared. The Manager accelerated and we were soon doing 110.

'At last! I've got the gum unstuck!' the other informed me. Then he turned sideways, stretched out his right foot, and half closed his eyes. Almost at once he pulled back his right leg and stretched out his left. As for me, yes, I was looking out the window as usual, enjoying the scenery but at the same time watching for his slightest movement. If he happened to make a suspicious move, in my left inside pocket I had my pistol.

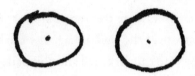

Two little circles, one next to the other. One of them, the right-hand one, a touch bigger. Not perfect circles. Somewhat irregular, tending to the elliptical.

He loosened his tie, which had been strangling him for hours. The knot was very tight. Then he considered bending down to tie his right shoelace, which he'd just noticed had come undone and was wriggling like a sea-snake. Ultimately, he didn't bend down, he did something else: he took the drawing he'd just made and held it far, then close, and scrutinised it carefully. Good! With two nervous pencil-strokes, he'd done it exactly as he wanted to. Two little circles, one next to the other. One of them, the right-hand one, a touch bigger. Not perfect circles. Somewhat irregular, tending to the elliptical.

He left the paper—he had nothing else to hand and had used the paper from his cigarette packet—beside the ashtray. A cheap battered aluminium one, advertising some company, probably an airline; he didn't notice.

When he'd gone into the Café Sport ten minutes earlier, he didn't sit at one of the many tables near the entrance; he headed straight to the far end of the large room.

Here the tables were free, apart from two or three. He chose one near the wall, up against the big rectangular mirror with the darkened and chipped gold frame. Two cherubs at the top of the frame, one facing the other: terribly kitsch. And chubby, as if they'd been overeating and taking vitamin B12. They were both blowing trumpets. Something metaphysical, no doubt. He turned his chair away from the mirror, not to have it constantly before his eyes, making him sick.

There was something else unfavourable about the spot he'd chosen: it was right by the toilet. And in spite of the notice, nicely written on a pink card and fixed with drawing-pins to the door

> DON'T FORGET TO CLOSE
> THE DOOR AFTER USE
> *The Management*

it was eternally open or half open. And it smelt. Not a lot, but it smelt.

He thought of getting up and changing location, but he couldn't be bothered to move. Anyway, it wasn't as if he'd be in the Café Sport for hours. The clock said 6.11, that antique hanging on the wall, its face all dusty with very curious marks, perhaps from flies. His own watch said thirteen minutes past. They'd arranged to meet at seven o'clock at the post office, in front of Foreign Reg-istered.

From the Café Sport to the post office was five min-utes at the most, but he'd go earlier to be first at their rendezvous. He wouldn't want ot be late and keep her waiting, nervously tapping her high heels or biting her nails. All on her own in the crowd that always swelled at that time of the evening in the post office, in the square, and in the side streets. And there were some types who, seeing a woman on her own, might try to make a pass.

'A brandy, a double. And a black pencil,' he'd said to the waiter, who had arrived to take his order before he'd even sat down.

The dour waiter didn't quite scratch his ear, as is usual or supposed to be usual in awkward situations, but said, 'A pencil? A black pencil?!' His manner was such that one might have expected him to say next, 'No, we don't serve pencils, sir!'

But in fact the waiter said no such thing. He searched, and searched again, and finally brought out from some pocket a black pencil bitten all over with the point half worn down.

'Don't look at it like that,' he reassured him, 'It does its job very well. Better still if you lick it.'

He had his pen in the right-hand pocket of his jacket, but he didn't want to draw with ink. Ink is neutral, expressionless. In such a medium, how could he express what he wanted to express? Two vigorous little circles. But a pencil is a warm, heart-felt thing.

The waiter took the order and disappeared. As for the brandy, it didn't appear.

He glanced half round the room. He saw some idle waiters. He clapped his hands to attract their attention. From his right, far off, he heard, 'At once, sir!' or something like it.

The sketch had come out right with the first attempt. Just as when he was a child he took coloured crayons and drew boats, birds, trees... No, he wasn't a child now. And the sketch wasn't a little boat. Nor a bird, nor a tree.

At last the waiter deigned to appear. In the distance, at the other end of the room. He saw him coming at his own pace, his tray full of coffees, drinks, and various things.

With a lightning move, he picked up the cheap aluminium ashtray and covered up his sketch so that it couldn't be seen. Immediately he changed his mind and pulled the ashtray aside, leaving the sketch in full view beside it. If the waiter or some third party happened to see and take note of the sketch, it was out of the question that he'd guess, even suspect, what those two little circles represented.

The first sip of the brandy tasted like her kiss a little earlier in his room.

He'd expected her at three, and at three she'd come. As soon as she'd come in, the door hardly closed, he took her, squeezed her, dissolved her, they glued themselves together mouth to mouth.

'Your kiss is somehow different!' he told her. 'A very strange taste. First time I've encountered it.'

'Yes?' she said, as if surprised. 'And tell me, my sweet, how do you find this new taste?'

'I'd say it was... very piquant!'

And he kissed her again. She slipped away from him and went to the mirror to fix her hair.

'Let me tell you that I've just come from the dentist. I went for a little filling. As for the taste you mention, which you find so piquant, it's the mouthwash, my sweet.'

The explanation spoilt his mood a bit, but it didn't take him long to get it back. When they fell into bed thirty seconds later, and struggled to undress each other, and slid off the bed onto the tiles, the shock of the tiles didn't cool their passion but...

He didn't even see him passing close to his table. But he felt it. And indeed, very markedly. Because in passing, this unknown customer of the Café Sport trod on his foot, the right one, which was sticking out a bit.

'You trod on me, sir,' he remarked.

Alarmed, the other stopped and looked at him.

'I did?' he said apologetically.

'Yes, you did! And it was my right foot, which...'

'Forgive me!' he interrupted. 'You see, I'm short-sighted. And I'm afraid lately it's got worse.'

'Alright then, if you are short-sighted...' he said, wanting to finish the conversation, terrified of the nonsense that bores talk in big—and indeed little—cafés, going on and on.

'May I put my cigarette out in your ashtray?' the man persisted.

He looked at him sideways. 'Yes, do.'

As soon as he was alone he took up the sketch again and looked at it from some distance, then he brought it close and bit it. He bit one circle, the smaller. On the left in the sketch.

The paper, imbued with tobacco, was very bitter. He took out his handkerchief and spat.

The urge to bite had come from an unconquerable force, a passion, to repeat what he'd done earlier, in his room. As they tussled on the now burning hot tiles, at some point he ended up on top of her and bit her breast. The smaller one, the right.

One by one, other tables around him were taken. This part of the café was warming up. Lots of conversation, lots of cigarettes, lots of people...

At the table under the antique hanging clock, three young people, one with a very neat moustache, were talking about *The Beauty of the Night*, the film that was showing at five central cinemas at the same time, and which had been getting and was still getting many favourable and unfavourable reviews. Both press and public were divided about it. Lots of fuss about *The Beauty of the Night* because of its daring—daring?—subject.

At the next table on the right, two middle-aged businessmen were talking very loudly and with expansive gestures about the price of cooking fat, which had fallen a few points recently. Or risen, he couldn't make it out. Their notebooks were dirty and greasy—as to be expected, since their business was cooking fat. They wrote in their notebooks, crossed things out, put in rows of numbers, and kept smoking and ordering more coffees. He noticed the hands of one of them; the fingers were very fat and lumpy, and he imagined they smelt of cooking fat.

At various other tables there were people alone. Loners. One with coffee, one with orange juice, one with nothing but himself.

In the corner were two older men who seemed to be army pensioners. They were looking covertly at photographs that one of them was taking out of his wallet—which was thick like a box, with a silvery monogram—to show the other.

They'll be risqué, he thought. *Nudes, strange positions, that sort of thing.*

It was twenty-five past by his watch. He'd leave soon, and at seven he'd meet her at the post office. It wasn't even an hour since they'd parted but he felt as if it had been months. He had such a longing to meet her!

In the two and a half months or so they'd been together, this was the first time he'd had her in his room. The first time they'd tussled. The first time he'd folded her in his arms, and in between his legs. The first time he'd ravished her breasts and bitten one.

The waiter brushed past his table again. No, he wasn't worried that the sketch was next to the ashtray, visible to anyone who passed. What should he worry about? How would a third party guess that those two little circles were her breasts?

He looked at his face in the mirror and adjusted his tie which had gone sideways. He saw the two cherubs, for all that he tried not to notice them. Or maybe *because* he tried not to notice them. He saw something else in the mirror: the scar below his right ear.

He'd been a pupil; one year more and he'd be leaving school. Just sixteen. How had fifteen whole years passed! Then he caught streptococcus, which settled at the root of his ear. There was an indescribable swelling. They cut it open and the pus came out; the scar was left. They told him to get it removed. He agreed, thought about going to get it done. Then he neglected it.

He took out his wallet to see if he had change for the brandy; the waiters usually complained if you offered a note, 'We haven't any change'—or so they say. Fortunately, he found change, but the waiter was at the other end of the room, as if he was on roller skates.

From the toilet stench that suddenly assailed him, he realised that someone else had come out and left the door open. He gave him an irritated look: a tall man, forty years old or so, with a neutral face. He thought of making some remark. *Maybe some people might learn manners and not leave the door wide open. Do they do that at home? There are others in the café; why should they have to breathe it in?*

But he said nothing to him. Why start an argument with a stranger? Especially as he was about to leave.

As this tall man passed by on his way out, he stood on his right foot—this was the second time it had happened, just as he was counting out change to leave on the saucer. No, he wouldn't let it go.

'You trod on me, sir.'

'I did?'

'Yes, and you trod on my right foot, which has a corn.'

'Really?' he said sarcastically, 'I thought it was the left,' and he went on his way without waiting for an answer.

'Twenty-eight minutes to seven,' he said to himself, 'Time to go.'

He saw a coin that had rolled to the foot of the table —was it his?—he bent to pick it up. 'Ah, yes, and the shoelace. I'd better tie it up, I might trip.'

He bent again for the shoelace, but didn't get there. One of the two cooking-fat salesmen, the one with the thick lumpy fingers, on his way to the toilet—or so it seemed—stopped at his table, leant over him, took out a yellow, laminated identity card and gently, very gently, almost tenderly, said to him:

'Special Branch.'

'I don't understand.'

'Leave the change for the brandy, and let's go! Get it right, it was a double.'

'I shall complain to your superiors!'

He got up and they set off between the tables.

'Lots of smoke in this café,' continued the agent as if they'd already been conversing. 'Lots of cigarettes, smoking the place up. Unhygienic atmosphere.'

It all happened so gently, so imperceptibly, that if one had asked the other customers they wouldn't have noticed anything.

Two metres from the exit he tripped over his shoelace.

'Can I stop and tie my shoelace?' he asked the agent. He gave no answer, but something in his eyes forbade further discussion.

nally all the arres ted suspects in Operation
Toilet Paper—all four—confessed, clearly, their
guilt. Another success for the Special Branch!

But I must make matters clear: the day before yesterday, in the morning, when our agents
led the four suspects to my office as soon as
they'd been caught to put them through a first
interrogation, before I had even prepared my
first question, one of the four, in spite of
the close watch kept by the guards, like lightning took a microscopic ampoule of cyanide from
his pocket, crushed it with his teeth, and that
was the end! I don't think it's necessary to go
into details about the death, that it was a
matter of seconds, etc. I at once reported the
matter to the Head Officer.

I wrote above, 'Finally all the arrested
suspects in Operation Toilet Paper—all four—

confessed, clearly, their guilt,' thus including the fourth suspect, even though I did* have
the opportunity to ask him even one question
and and get an answer. But what, after all, is
his suicide? Is it not a clear confession of
his guilt?

    *not

He stopped and read over the piece from the beginning of page two, which he'd just typed. It was OK, except that he'd typed 'and' twice. He typed XXX over
the extra one and continued.

    I consider it expedient to give, first,
shortly but fully, the story of Operation Toilet Paper, and then proceed to details of the
questioning.
    The day before yesterday, the 14th of
September, at the station, where the 11.05 had
arrived, porters were unloading various goods
from the luggage van.
    At one moment, as three wooden crates marked
'Toilet Paper' were being unloaded, one box
slipped from the hands of the porter and
crashed onto the concrete platform, splitting
open at one corner from which hundreds of
leaflets against the Regime spilt out.
    The agents of the Special Branch who were
completing their usual investigations at the

```
station and the area around it lost no time.
Result: four suspects caught at once.
   The other two crates were opened and it was
ascertained that none of the three contained a
single roll of toilet paper but only proclama-
```

He changed the typing paper

— 3 —

```
tions—in total 4,310—with the same text against
the Regime.
```

He made a careful check of what he had typed so far of his report. Nothing to correct. But the 'a' didn't come out clearly, and it annoyed him because 'a' is the most frequently used letter. He'd known that for years, ever since he'd been a child and had a passion, a mania, for solving cryptograms wherever he could find them. Who would have suspected at the time that years later, almost as soon as he'd got his law degree, he'd apply to be an investigator in the Special Branch? An apprentice at first, in accordance with the regulations, and in record time, thanks to his unusual powers and the zeal he showed, a permanent employee. He dealt with cryptograms all the time, and the many and various mysteries in the struggles of the Special Branch to protect the Regime, a duty which fell exclusively to them.

With the little brush he very carefully cleaned the 'a', and also the 'A', even though the latter didn't come out fuzzy.

When he happened to have written an interrogation report quickly, he was in the habit of typing it out himself. He was hoping to perfect his touch-typing.

```
The four suspects were brought at once to
the Special Branch and at the orders of the
Head Officer I carried out the interrogation
myself.
    In detail, the interrogation and the result
I achieved were as follows: the suspects con-
fessed their guilt and
```

He looked it over. The 'a' was OK. Perfectly clear.

He made to continue, but didn't proceed. That unbelievable stomach pain came over him. Like a finger prodding his stomach hard. He'd had it these last few days, since last Wednesday.

It was the first time in all his thirty-five years that he'd had trouble in his stomach. He always said he had an iron stomach, and was proud of it. Now the pain had appeared and hadn't left him in peace for a single day since Wednesday. It lasted only seconds, and then disappeared. What could it be? Nerves. It seemed to him it was probably one of those things they call 'psychosomatic'. In the office they always had a load of work, interrogations one after the other. Especially recently, they'd come thick and fast—but when hadn't they? On the one hand there were interrogations that only let him leave the Special Branch office late at night, or in the morning after an all-night session, when he would leave limp with fatigue just to change clothes, wash, and then go back to the office. On the other hand, the innumerable coffees and one cigarette after another.

His wife took the matter more seriously. She shouted at him to go and get it seen to at once, not to neglect his health, etc., etc. Certainly he'd go, given time and inclination. Above all inclination.

As soon as the pain left him, he took a few paces to get rid of the numbness in his legs.

He went to the window. Why was it closed? September this year was unusually warm. He opened both panes wide and went straight back to his desk; the aspirin were in the third drawer on the left. That headache that had been torturing him since the afternoon was too much.

There was still half a glass of water left that accompanied the coffee—the fifteenth or the sixteenth?—he'd just drunk. Aspirin and glass in his hand, he went back to the window.

The Theatre Square, onto which the Special Branch office looked, was decorated with lights. Lots of them, and multi-coloured. He looked at some of the advertisements that flashed on and off, looked at the traffic in the square and down the four avenues running off the square like four fingers. And took his aspirin. The moment he brought it to his lips, he thought of the suspect with the cyanide. He'd made just such a movement.

'Though it wasn't aspirin! When all's said and done, our friend got away from us. A fine trick. He took the easy way out.'

There was no more time to stay at the window. The Chief wanted him to bring the report on Operation Toilet Paper by eleven at the latest and it was already 10.20.

He took a cigarette from the heap he had in front of him, then changed his mind; he'd smoke it later.

```
                    yet another organisation
against the Regime was dissolved in its in-
fancy. The Special Branch
```

'Are you there?' the voice of the Chief came over the intercom.

'Yes, I'm finishing the report on Operation Toilet Paper and you'll have it—'

'It's not about the report!' he interrupted. 'Operation Toilet Paper has been definitively closed and can be filed. Now I want you for an operation that's just started, Operation Café Sport. Four hours ago, at about six thirty, our agents picked up two suspects. One in the

Café Sport and the other outside on the pavement. I'll give you the details when you bring the report to my office. I just wanted you to know that I need you for this new thing. Ah, yes, and you'll set out in the morning, at precisely seven o'clock, for the capital. And by the usual route: car and ferry. You and the Manager will bring one of the two to Central, the other has been on his way already for half an hour or more.'

'At last!' shouted the Manager. 'He's deigned to let us pass. The beast!' He'd just managed, with a truly startling manoeuvre, to escape from the annoying grey-green coach, which for ages had been trying—you'd say deliberately—to block their way.

'The Manager's a maestro!' he said to the Interrogator, as if asking his opinion. 'I called him the Manager, but what could I do? I hear you call him the Manager all the time.'

'And why not?' the Interrogator agreed. 'In the Special Branch everyone calls him the Manager. He got the nickname because in every conversation, even the most trivial, he says, "Me, when I was a manager..."'

'Manager of what?' he asked.

'Fleas!' cut in the person in question.

'Come now!' he said as if he thought we were pulling his leg.

'Yes, a flea manager,' the Interrogator assured him.

'For eight years running I had my own troupe,' the Manager informed him. 'My act, the Great Flea Revue, left its mark on all the variety theatres. An amazing spectacle. First appearance in international fleadom. That's what you'd call success! It broke my heart when the force of circumstance caused the troupe to disband. A mysterious microbe turned everything upside down; all the members of the troupe caught it, one by one. Chief actors, bit parts, technical staff. And I found myself a manager without a troupe! So I went and became an agent in the Special Branch. Why not?'

'I would never have thought it,' he said, as if he were to blame for not knowing.

'A manager of fleas!' the Manager continued. Suddenly he turned the wheel to the left, very nearly hitting a motorcycle that was rushing past. Our man fell against the Interrogator. It looked as if he was scratching himself on his shoulder.

'Excuse me!' he said.

'No problem! What with the struggling with the wheel the Manager was obliged to do, we lost our balance.'

'No, it's something else. You see, when I hear talk of fleas... if I just happen to hear the word "flea", I start itching right away. The same if I happen to see the word "flea" written or printed. There, now that I've said the word, and heard it, I'm itching.' And he scratched himself on the Interrogator's shoulder again.

'Very strange!' he said with a sidelong glance.

'Isn't it funny? Funny and dramatic at the same time!'

'An allergy!' was the Manager's opinion.

'An allergy, what else?' he agreed. 'But the most surprising thing is that I start to itch only when I hear or read the word.'

'You mean?'

'Well, I don't have the slightest problem if a whole army of them is crawling over me...'

'What strange things happen in the world!' said the Manager. 'And to think that I was fooling you with what I said before. I wasn't a manager... of what I said before, no! I was a manager in wrestling matches!'

They all fell silent.

'You told me the ferry leaves at 11.10,' he said, breaking the silence. 'And the next one?'

'The next one's tomorrow morning at 6.20,' said the Interrogator.

'Well, haven't you been to the capital by this route before?' said the Manager, joining the conversation.

'No. It's the first time I've been to the capital by car and ferry. Up to now, every time I've had to go to the capital—not so often—I've always taken the train.'

'The train!' said the Manager. 'Such a bother. And one-and-a-half hour's journey.'

'I had no idea this way was so handy. I'll use it in future. So, there's no boat later, in the evening?'

'The schedule is two a day,' the Interrogator informed him. 'One in the early morning, 6.20, and one at 11.10. The two in the afternoon have been cancelled for now.'

'I hope we have no delays and get to the capital this evening, to get this business over with! Go to Central, let them see they've got nothing on me and set me free.'

'Don't worry,' the Manager assured him. 'We'll be in time for the ferry and the rest. I have complete faith in our car.'

'And in our driver!' our man added.

'You'll see *me* at the wheel later,' said the Interrogator. 'The Manager and I agreed to share the driving. The Manager from town to the ferry, and from when we leave the ferry to the capital, me. You'll have the chance to see who drives better.'

'OK. I can assure you of one thing: my judgement will be completely impartial.'

There was a noise and the Manager, complaining, drove at once onto the right-hand verge and braked.

'Fine time to have something go wrong!' said the Interrogator nervously. 'What do we do if we get stuck?'

'Let's see what's wrong first,' said the Manager, and got out, opened the bonnet, and poked around inside.

'What's wrong, tell us what's wrong!' shouted the Interrogator, who hadn't moved from his seat.

'I told you to wait!' answered the Manager, leaning over the engine. 'Don't be impatient!'

'It'll be very bad luck if there's a problem,' our man said. 'You understand—I hope you understand—I want us to get to the capital as quickly as possible, and at least get this business over with by this evening!'

'I can't say yes or no,' said the Manager, emerging from under the bonnet. 'It's a mystery! Everything seems OK, but there's something... I can't make out what. Anyway, we'll carry on. Maybe it's nothing serious.'

He got into the car, wiped his oily hands, took out a piece of chewing gum—this time he didn't offer any to the others—and started the engine.

'It's a good thing the Manager didn't find anything,' our man said. 'It would be nerve-racking for me if we didn't get to Central by evening. I want to get it over with as quickly as possible. It's quite enough!'

'Let's hope everything goes well and we'll be in time for the ferry,' said the Manager.

They fell silent again. It was a pleasant interval. The heat, and the boredom of the journey, were taking their toll. Ten minutes or a quarter of an hour of silence brought them back on form. As if they'd had a shower and felt refreshed.

My report on Operation Toilet Paper took altogether six and a quarter pages. I looked it over a final time, quickly but carefully, corrected a few small mistakes, the usual oversights. Then I collated the four copies. Ah, yes, when I type my reports I make a top sheet and three copies. According to the rules, interrogation reports are typed in quadruplicate. The top copy goes to Central. As for the other three: one for the Chief, one for local Special Branch archives, and one for the Interrogator's personal records.

I signed all four—initialling every page—and took up the Chief's copy. As I closed the door I turned and switched off the light, as is my habit. I don't want light in my office when I'm not there.

The Chief's office was two floors up, fifth floor, number 560. So I wanted to take the lift, but all three were in use. To avoid delay, I went up the stairs.

When I knocked I wasn't sure if I heard the 'Yes!' that the Chief usually calls out. I took the initiative and went in. He'd called me in, after all. I saw the Chief and the Manager—the two of them alone in the office—standing over by the window, and it seemed to me they were having a confidential talk; they stopped when I appeared.

'I'm afraid I came at the wrong moment,' I said. 'Shall I go away and come back again?'

'No, don't come back again!' said the Chief curtly, taking off his glasses as if to see me with the naked eye.

I saw him take his handkerchief from his back trouser pocket, where he always keeps it, and clean his glasses very carefully.

I'd heard long ago, completely by chance, that the Chief was astigmatic, but I can't be sure, because I'd also heard, again quite by chance, that he was neither astigmatic nor short-sighted nor anything, and that those glasses, which he always wore, did nothing, that is, they were plain glass, like the glasses actors wear when they play the part of someone with glasses. I had no idea why he should wear such glasses, and I had no reason to have any idea. No! In the Special Branch, everything was confidential. In the double-bolted archives, where all the information concerning those guilty or suspected of being guilty of actions against the Regime, or of being ideologically unsympathetic to the Regime, were filed away, well, in those archives everything was secret. The walls, the corridors, the stairs, the lifts, the inner court-yard, the roof, the windows, the balconies, the toilets, all secret. For example, it was quite possible that in a toilet cistern they'd put a super-sensitive—the only kind of sensitivity allowed in the Special Branch—micro-phone, to catch all kinds of noises, from those usually heard in a toilet to voices in monologue or dialogue.

No, I had no reason to have any idea whether the Chief really had astigmatism or not, because the funda-mental, the number one thing for a Special Branch agent was to thirst for, to risk his life for information about everything that happened *outside* the Special Branch, and to be indifferent to all that happened *inside* the Special Branch.

'I mean to say, don't leave at all!' the Chief explained when he'd finished cleaning his glasses. 'And since there's no question of your leaving, there's none of your coming back. You and I and the Manager have to talk about Operation Café Sport, which I just told you about.'

'Anyway, I have my report on Operation Toilet Paper. It came to six pages and—'

He waved my remarks away with his hand, took the report and, without even looking at it, left it on his desk. On the right, near the telephone.

'Agreed.' he said. 'I accept your report on Operation Toilet Paper, but as far as Special Branch is concerned, that operation is over. If either of you wants to sit down, please do. Now I must tell you the story of Operation Café Sport.'

He remained standing, and neither of us sat down.

'All this happened today,' he began, 'The story began in the morning, at eleven, when I received a letter, posted yesterday. This is the envelope:'

PERSONAL

```
To the Head Officer
of the Special Branch—Local
```

'Here is the letter, typed on the same machine:'

```
At the Café Sport tomorrow afternoon, the 16th
inst., at 6.15—6.30, someone who is an impor-
tant member of an organisation against the
Regime will enter and sit down. He is com-
pletely unknown to the Special Branch up to
now. Neither he, nor the organisation in ques-
tion. His photograph is enclosed. I'm sorry the
photograph is not very recent, but it is, I
think and hope, sufficiently clear for the Spe-
cial Branch should you decide to interest your-
selves in him or the man who plans to meet him
in the Café Sport. What you do with this infor-
mation is of no concern to me.—
```

'And here's the photograph.'

We examined the photograph. It didn't mean anything to us. A completely ordinary face, such as one
meets by the thousand. Without question it was someone in particular, this unknown man with the big glasses,
the big ears—the big ear—and the thick moustache.
With such a photograph in his hands, a Special Branch
agent would be able to pick the person out from even a
hundred customers of the Café Sport.

'That's how Operation Café Sport started,' continued
the Chief.

There was a knock at the door and at the Chief's
'Yes!' an agent came in.

'What's happening?' the Chief asked rather abruptly,
'I hope you haven't come to tell me that one of the two
people arrested at the Café Sport has committed suicide.
The unforeseen incident with the fourth person in Operation Toilet Paper who slipped out of our hands was
quite enough.'

'No, it's not a matter of suicide,' said the agent. 'The man we're holding has complained. He says he should have been questioned here in the presence of the other one.'

The Chief smiled. 'Calm him down,' he instructed the agent. 'Remind him of exactly what I told him a little while ago; that the time is not far off when the two of them will be interrogated together, the one facing the other. It's just that that will happen at Central.'

The agent left.

'What was I telling you? Oh, yes. What was I supposed to do with this letter? Ignore it? No! Right away our agents took up their positions at the Café Sport. They sat at various tables, some outside on the pavement, others inside. One by one, or two or three together at one table. And they waited. What else should they do? All they had was the photograph, of which we'd made lots of copies. Meanwhile, needless to say, they scrutinised the customers; did they or did they not look like the man in the photograph? At 6.12 the man in question made his appearance. Not quite like the photograph; a little older and with a different hairstyle. Anyway, there was no doubt that he was the one we were waiting for. He sat at a table on the right as you go in, near the big window looking onto the avenue. He ordered an orange juice. "Well chilled!" he told the waiter. Then he calmly drank his juice with a straw. Like someone who wasn't in any hurry. He opened the newspaper, which he'd asked the waiter for, looked at it, probably not carefully. He finished his juice—he left a little—got up and went to the toilet. A technical difficulty... In two minutes, at 6.29 precisely, our man came out of the toilet and moved between the tables towards the exit. Our agents watched closely! When he was level with the third table, he tripped on someone's right foot, stepping on it. He didn't take any notice and continued towards the exit. But the other man was annoyed and called, "You trod on me, sir!". Finally, the unknown man in the photograph had the goodness to stop. "Me?" he asked in surprise. "Yes, you! And you trod on my right foot, which has a corn!" Then he looked at him ironically and said, "Really. Believe me, I thought it was the left." Going straight to the exit, he went out onto Independence Avenue turning left, and behind him two agents were waiting to see if he would meet someone else, so they could arrest both. In the end, he didn't meet anyone, so he was arrested on his own at the entrance of the Star Cinema. As for the other one, with the corn on his right foot, his accomplice—he was the only person he came into contact with, albeit seemingly innocently—he was arrested by one of our agents. There were two at one table and they pretended to be cooking-fat salesmen. And so, these two partners in crime came into our hands. I myself did the interrogation. Who would you like me to start with? Let's take the man with the corn on his right foot first. What d'you think of this?'

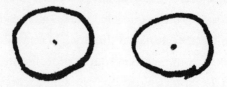

'Two little circles,' I said, taking hold of the paper— paper from a cigarette packet—which the Chief suddenly produced from a dossier on his desk.

'And what do you say?' asked the Manager.

'I agree with the Interrogator. It's exactly that: two little circles.'

The Chief made a gesture like waving away smoke, and said, 'Those two little circles you see, and which I saw, too, may of course be nothing more than two little circles. That's to say, it's not impossible they have no secret conspiratorial meaning. Just a simple sketch. For example, he who made the sketch, the one whose right foot was trodden on, when he sat down in the Café Sport asked the waiter for a double brandy and a black pencil. The waiter gave him the pencil, and then, taking the paper from his cigarette packet, the suspect drew the two little circles—it's not out of the question that our man made two little circles completely by chance, to pass the time, rather than making two little squares or something similar. But the exact opposite is also not out of the question: that the sketch has a special meaning, something we don't know at present. But better to take things in order. As I told you earlier, our agents went to the Café Sport much earlier than the time, 6.15–6.30, that the anonymous letter states. And waiting for the man in the photograph to turn up, they followed everyone and everything in the café. So they noticed the man with the corn on his right foot. They saw how he came in and went and sat at a table far inside, in front of the big mirror that's there. He ordered the double brandy and the black pencil. Anyway, you already know the circumstances. He made the sketch, and at one moment he bent down and smelt it. Smelt it or bit it, our agents couldn't see clearly, two customers had stopped between the tables to talk and were blocking their view. One of the two so-called cooking-fat salesmen, I should add, arrested our man a little later, when he was quite sure he'd had contact, however innocent, with the unknown man in the photograph. As they left, our man and the agent left the sketch on the table. However, the other cooking-fat salesman picked it up. No, our man didn't seem disturbed that they'd arrested him, he just said, "I don't understand" and "I shall complain to your superiors." Oh, and yes, he asked permission from the agent to tie his right shoelace. Why such a carefree attitude? Was he guilty and brazen about it, was he acting a part, or was he, on the other hand, innocent and calm through his innocence? Let's put the question to one side and continue with the facts. He smelt or bit the sketch with the two circles, we said that earlier. We're not sure exactly what he did. Perhaps it was a nervous tic. Or maybe something else: you know, there are people who have a passion for smelling various things, for example, printed paper—freshly printed, of course; printers' ink gives them special satisfaction. Or they might smell women's underwear. Anyway, that sketch with the two circles, which our man left on the table as he was taken away—did he forget it, or did he abandon it deliberately so that it wouldn't fall into our hands?—well, the other agent, the other one who was discussing the price of cooking fat, took it immediately. As for the suspect in the photograph, as you know, two agents followed him: they let him leave the Café Sport, turn left on Independence Avenue, and finally, in front of the Star Cinema, they arrested him. So he, too, was brought under our authority. Now we must temporarily go back to the other, so as not to lose continuity. After his arrest, they brought the double-brandy-and-sketch man here. In a Special Branch car, which was parked two blocks away from the Café Sport. All the way he showed calm, complete sangfroid. Just once, as they passed through Post Office Square, he turned and looked at his watch; maybe he had some reason. Anyway, he told the agent who asked him if he looked at his watch because he had some rendezvous that no, he had no rendezvous, he'd just looked automatically. They took him first to the usual room on the third floor and left him to wait. Meanwhile, to cover all eventualities—

let us not forget the suspect in Operation Toilet Paper and the cyanide ampoule—they told him to undress completely, suit, underwear, shoes and watch. They gave him other clothes, and they searched his very carefully. Here's what we found in his pockets.'

And, taking what items they'd found on the man from the Café Sport one by one from his desk, he showed them to us and named them:

'One packet of cigarettes, nine cigarettes in total, that's to say eleven are gone, and the paper from the packet which I told you he'd taken out in the Café Sport to draw the two little circles. His identity card with all his details; first name and surname, name of father, name of mother, age thirty-two years—he's thirty-one, they put one year too many—unmarried, profession self-employed, address Nikis Street 120A. Another identity card, from the travel and tourist agency Hermes where he works. A nail-clipper. Two condoms. Wallet, containing only money and no sign that could shed any light on the matter for us. A purse with coins. In short, nothing special from the point of view of the investigation was found.'

'Other facts? Information? House search?'

'Everything was done as it should be,' the Chief told me, 'From the moment they brought him here at the greatest possible speed. Nothing was found against him. At his house—a ground floor room with its own entrance and toilet—a fruitless search. All the information we've got from other residents, neighbours, others working at Hermes—it took an hour to complete enquiries—all point to the same conclusion: a placid man. He has not otherwise come to the attention of the Special Branch or the police. Until now he's not given the slightest suspicion of activity against the Regime, or simply being not in favour of the Regime. I took him for interrogation two hours after he'd been brought to Special Branch. I told him straight away that the other man, his accomplice, had already explained their meeting in the Café Sport and I asked him to tell me his side of it. He calmly told me he didn't know the other man, that they were not partners in crime, and that their meeting in the café had no significance; that it was completely by chance. I asked what the two of them said when he trod on his right foot. With no hesitation he told me the dialogue word for word, an apparently innocent dialogue. I will give you details later which I leave out for the moment because I want to paint a general picture. Well, maybe you understand the trick I was playing: my agents had heard the dialogue in its entirety, they didn't miss a word. I already knew the dialogue, but I pretended not to, in order to see if he would have the honesty to give it to me complete or if he would make changes. In that second case, we would have something specific against him. Then I asked him the meaning of the two little circles he'd drawn on the paper from his cigarette packet. I showed him the sketch; he didn't

seem surprised that we had it in our possession. He gave
me the following answer: "They have no meaning,
they're exactly what you see: two little circles. Don't
tell me those two little circles are suspicious! I drew
them to pass the time; instead of two little circles I
could have drawn two little squares or two little rect-
angles or something." I told him I couldn't accept this
explanation and it wasn't out of the question that the
two seemingly innocent little circles were a plan: two
armouries with weapons intended for use against the
Regime. He laughed and told me, looking me straight
in the eye: "I'm a peace-loving citizen." It was then that
I answered, "For the Regime, 'peace-loving citizen'
means nothing. Nothing! The population is divided
into those who are for the Regime and those who aren't.
To be an enemy of the Regime, you don't have to have
done something against it; it's enough that you're not
from the Regime, that you have not done anything that
shows positively that you are *from* the Regime. Yes, for
the Regime the rule 'He who is not with us is against
us' applies." He listened to me carefully, but didn't
change his stance in any way. It's not necessary just now
to give you all the details of the interrogation; I'll return
to the subject. I'll confine myself for the moment to in-
forming you that from start to finish the suspect kept
his sangfroid, an appearance of innocence. The only
thing he asked was that he should be questioned face-
to-face with the other as soon as possible. I told him

yes, as soon as the individual interrogations were over, there would be a face-to-face questioning. Meanwhile I was in constant contact with Central. They explained to me that Operation Café Sport was of immediate and great interest to them. I had repeated telephone conversations with Central from the time I first phoned to tell them about Operation Café Sport and the facts on the two suspects. At intervals I telephoned or was telephoned by Central about the progress of the interrogation, and its first conclusions. As for my interrogation of the man with the double brandy, I stopped it at one point and continued three quarters of an hour later. At about ten, I brought him up again and asked if he had anything new to declare; he told me no, all that he had to declare he had declared already. Then I announced, "But I have something new to tell you: tomorrow morning, very early, we shall take you by Special Branch car to Central. Your accomplice is already on the way, accompanied, of course, on orders from Central, based on what we have found out so far. Therefore the face-to-face interrogation with your accomplice will take place in Central. I have no further involvement with Operation Café Sport; it is now in the hands of Central." I couldn't say he was pleased with the news. On the contrary, he showed clearly that the dragging out of the affair was getting on his nerves. He said something about unwarranted trouble, and the conversation ended there.'

'So, tomorrow he'll be taken to Central,' said the Manager.

'Yes. That's to say, the two of you will take him. You'll leave very early: you must set out at seven to catch the ferry at 11.10.'

'The microfilm's ready!' the person in charge of photography informed the Chief over the intercom. 'It's all clear, by unusual good luck. You can see it as soon as you like.'

'I bet it's going to rain,' said the Manager. Or, he said, 'I bet it's not going to rain.'

I didn't hear which of the two.

'What exactly did you say about rain?' I asked him.

'I was making a weather forecast: "Rain in the outlook."'

'You don't say!' I remarked ironically.

'Why, please? You have some objection?'

I laughed loudly. 'Well, what put the idea of rain in your head? The sun's been roasting us continually and there are no clouds up there. No, there are two or three little ones, innocent in appearance and as diaphanous as women's nylon underwear. But to talk seriously of rain is going too far!'

The Manager made a gesture. At first I thought he was waving away a fly, but I couldn't see any fly, and then I realised his gesture meant he disagreed with me.

'This stifling heat!' he said almost at once. 'Don't forget we're in the middle of September, and such stifling heat is not at all natural. Don't you agree?'

'The Manager's right,' the man from the Café Sport joined in. 'It's my opinion, though I didn't say anything before, that this stifling heat is very strange. I think it'll end in rain.'

'So we're two to one,' I said. 'You are in the majority.'

We were going at a steady 110. I lit a cigarette and thought how undeniable, how realistic was the Chief's philosophy. Like an algebra theorem: 'He who is not with us is against us.' The Regime is the line separating us from them. Whoever is for the Regime has his place here; whoever is not with the Regime has his place there. Between the two banks, the abyss.

'Knowing our luck, our bad luck, I mean,' continued the Manager, 'I'm very much afraid we shall be late.'

'Now that I've reconsidered the question,' I said, 'It's indeed strange that it's so hot, and an unpleasant heat. It's not impossible that this stifling heat is cooking up some rain.'

'With the first squall, the traffic gets disturbed. And if there's a traffic jam, we're in danger of losing valuable time. Anyway, to avoid skidding I'll have to slow down.'

'That's true,' I agreed. 'We'll have to quit the 110 we're doing.'

The Manager adjusted his trilby, which kept falling down, then hunched over the wheel as if he wanted to give it all his attention. The truth is the road couldn't be more congested.

The other one, the one in between us, had such a bland air one might have thought he was under anaesthetic. Or maybe he was simply sleepy, and that was why he seemed drugged. Indeed, his right eye was half closed.

From the time he'd fallen into the hands of the Special Branch and the process of interrogation had begun, our man was automatically on the other shore. He was unable to prove that he was with the Regime, therefore he was against it. The Regime's enemy—and mine.

'The road surface becomes a nightmare with the rain,' he said, looking from me to the Manager. 'It's as slippery as if it had been greased.'

'I'm soaked in sweat,' the Manager complained.

'Me too,' I added. 'My shirt's sticking to me, especially round the collar. It's like Elastoplast. And my underwear, it's a nuisance.'

'My hands are sticky, greasy,' said the other.

In my mind's eye I saw him with his right hand raised—or maybe his left—saying to the Chief, 'I'm a peace-loving citizen.' They all start like that, or most of them anyway, when we catch them and bring them to the Special Branch for interrogation. They play the dead bed-bug, the dove of peace—'I'm a peace-loving citizen' is their tune. As if they had no idea how useless this was. It doesn't work. If you've done nothing positive for the Regime, just being 'a peace-loving citizen' doesn't merely mean nothing, on the contrary it counts against you. They should pass a law as soon as possible to punish as a particular crime being 'a peace-loving citizen' when one can't show evidence of being with the Regime. And furthermore, the same law should make it an offence even to offer the defence of 'I'm a peace-loving citizen'. Because he who is no more than 'a peace-loving citizen' is at the same time a lawbreaker.

At the 133 kilometre post on National Route 40, the Manager got chewing gum out and offered it to us. I took some gratefully; for some time I'd had such a thirst that my tongue was like a dried potato. I was going to ask him for some but he anticipated me.

'No thanks!' The other refused the chewing gum. 'I hope you won't misunderstand me if I refuse—well, I've already refused—this time. The piece you gave me a while ago got stuck in a bad tooth. The one before the last on the upper right. It's been rotten for some time...'

'... and when water or food gets on it, it drives you crazy,' the Manager added. 'I've got one the same. I overheard when you were explaining it to my colleague.'

My first acquaintance with the Chief was seven years ago, when I first joined the Special Branch as an apprentice interrogator and in five months I was made permanent—record time! Normally it takes three years. I was full of pride and joy when I read the following in Central's daily orders, the ones that made me permanent: '...in view of the unusual power and zeal shown as an apprentice, and taking into account the passion he has for the Regime, and...' Well, from my first contact with the Chief, I understood what a powerful personality he is! His influence on me, direct and indirect, then and now, has been strong and deep. His thought has entered my very marrow—that's to say, the total lack of thought.

What the Chief said—a milestone in my life—when we eight trainee interrogators saw him in turn to take our oaths, is engraved in my consciousness: 'You are obliged to recognise that for the Special Branch and for those who serve it, a completely different philosophy applies. People, according to this philosophy, are not divided into good and bad, honourable and dishonourable and other such pointless and useless divisions left over from the past. An interrogator for the Special Branch recognises one and only one division: for the Regime and not for the Regime. This simplification is very valuable both for the Special Branch and for each of you individually. The secret, the key to success and inner peace, both for the Regime and for the individual, is this simplification: the less your thinking operates, the happier you will be and the more useful to the Regime. The number one danger is thinking. Don't make lots of distinctions; no inner dialogues with yourself. The one and only distinction, I emphasise, permitted to an interrogator in the Special Branch is the following: with the Regime or not with the Regime.' Such was my emotion when I heard the Chief—it was in the afternoon, June, June the 11th—that even the stomach ache I had from stuffing myself with a kilo of cherries at lunchtime, even that stomach ache, couldn't mar my enthusiasm. Tears came to my eyes and at once I took off the dark glasses I'd bought in the morning specially for my career. If I'd left them on, the Chief would certainly have been unable to see my tears.

'Shall we put some music on?' the Manager suggested. 'It's 10.12. Until half past there's "Music for All" on.'

'Good idea!' I agreed. I leant down to the radio and, not without effort—there was a lot of interference— managed to catch the station. It was weird modern stuff.

The Manager said, 'These modern rhythms are in my blood, all lively, lots of movement.'

'Well, modern rhythms do nothing for me,' our man said shortly and looked sideways at the Manager as if he thought he might have gone too far.

'You did well to give your opinion straight out,' I encouraged him. 'The Manager has his opinion, and you yours, and me mine, and mine, perhaps, agrees with... the Manager's? No, I'm of your opinion. To hell with this modern, meaningless stuff with meaningless rhythms! What's your taste in music?'

'The old romantic songs.'

'Bravo!' I gave my enthusiasm full rein. 'I'd say we had the same tastes.'

'What time d'you expect to get to the capital?' he asked me.

'Well, 11.10 we leave on the ferry... two and a half hours at sea. About one thirty, or quarter to two, we get off the ferry, then three hours in the car... five o'clock, or just after five, we should be at our destination.'

'Wonderful! Early enough for me to be finished at Central today. And then I'll invite you and the Manager for a drink at some night spot. The capital has a lively night life and I suggest all three of us go to enjoy it.'

'So, you're sure they'll let you go at Central,' I said. 'And straight away, too.'

'Yes! There's nothing against me. As for the other chap, he's completely unknown to me, as they'll realise when the two of us are questioned together. He can't make something out of nothing. I'll stop his talk. My adventure will be over by tonight, as soon as we get to Central.'

I didn't say any more. Nor did the Manager, who perhaps had heard what he said. I turned towards the windscreen and tidied up my bunch of flowers.

Then the Manager started to laugh. A mystery: nothing happened to provoke such an outburst. We weren't even talking just then—it was one of our frequent silences.

'What's up with you to make you laugh like that?' I asked him.

'There, to our left, that refrigerator lorry,' he said in between guffaws.

A refrigerator lorry with nothing out of the ordinary about it. Silver-coloured, the way they usually paint aeroplanes; we were driving alongside it.

'Well? What's up with the lorry to make you burst out laughing?'

'Can't you see what's written on it?'

I looked again, and saw written on the side, low down, in badly-written capitals:

FROZEN FISH
POSEIDON
FRESHER THAN FRESH

'Isn't it funny?' continued the Manager. 'That "Fresher than Fresh Fish". I don't know; at least I find it very amusing,' and he underlined what he'd said with a fresh burst of laughter.

'Yes, it is rather odd,' said the Café Sport man, 'but not so very funny.'

'OK, you have your opinion and I have mine,' the Manager insisted. 'And it reminds me, my wife expects me to return from the capital with some fish fresh from the harbour. And the petticoat.'

'What petticoat?' I asked.

'Well, she saw an advertisement in some magazine for some new sort of petticoat they have in the capital. She gave me the address, I put it in my pocket—if I didn't leave it behind. I don't know what sort of petticoat they are; something special about them. I'll be in trouble if I forget her orders!'

'Don't worry,' the Café Sport man said, 'I'll make a point of reminding you. Fish and petticoats.'

'Your services gratefully accepted. You mean, you're sure you'll clear things up with Central in no time?'

'But of course! There's nothing against me. The people at Central will realise at once that I've been put to this trouble for nothing. And they'll apologise, too.'

'It's not out of the question,' I said.

We'd just passed the 214-kilometre marker when the Manager turned and said, 'What the hell's the engine doing? I'll pull over to see what's up.'

I stayed in the car—I couldn't very well leave our man alone. Anxiously, I watched the Manager open the bonnet and bend over the engine.

'What bad luck we're having today,' I moaned, 'What with one delay after the other, we're in danger of missing the ferry.'

'Well, you'd better cross out the ferry,' said the Manager, emerging all smudged from the engine.

'What are you trying to say?'

'Don't get excited!' he continued. 'It's perfectly simple: the distributor is no longer any use to us.'

'The hell it isn't!' I shouted, and went and punched the wing of the car.

'We've had it now. You saw I was worried earlier that something was wrong with the engine. Now I know what it is: the distributor.'

'Take care while I look at the engine myself.'

He took a couple of paces towards our man, and then I bent to look at the engine, looking it over for some time, at least ten minutes.

'You're right,' I said, coming out, 'Out of the question to go so much as half a metre further. As if anyone would expect us to get stuck because of the distributor!'

'And it's ten to, already. The ferry leaves in a quarter of an hour, and we'll have to wait until tomorrow morning.'

'Aren't you going to say anything?' I turned to the other. 'Why are you just sitting there with that superior attitude?'

Glued to his seat, he stared at me like a rabbit in the headlights.

'What should I say?' he muttered. 'I think *I'm* the unluckiest of us.'

A traffic policeman on his motorbike chose just that moment to turn up. He drew right up to us and parked his bike next to the car. 'What's going on here?' he asked and at once pulled out his booklet to give us a ticket. He stared hard at each of us suspiciously.

'The distributor!' the Manager told him.

'Meaning?' he asked as if he'd never heard of a distributor.

'Our distributor's had it,' I explained calmly, though ready to burst with frustration. 'The distributor's broken and we can't move another inch.'

'Oh yes?' he said and stared at us as if we were exotic beasts, dinosaurs or some such.

At last he made as if to close his booklet and leave, but changed his mind and got off his bike, stretching and doing his early morning exercises. Then he approached the Manager. 'Hot today,' he remarked. 'Well, the distributor... let me have a look, see what's happened to it.'

'Help yourself!' said the Manager. 'You think we stopped in the middle of the main road just because we fancied it?'

At that moment the walkie-talkie on his bike called him and the traffic policeman gave up his examination and went to answer it.

'Yes, I'm at 214. No, nothing important. Private car stopped because of a faulty distributor. What? Crash at 305? OK, I'm on my way.'

Then he turned to us.

'Find a garage to fetch your car, and quickly!'

He got on his bike, choking us with exhaust fumes as he left.

Our attempts to thumb a lift were fruitless.

'Three of us, a whole crowd. Who's going to stop and take us?' said the Manager.

'Look who's talking!' the Interrogator exclaimed. 'With your long hair—how often d'you get it cut?—and your sideburns, you're a perfectly suspicious character.'

'So, it's me who spoilt everything? Is that what you're saying?'

Just then a lorry was good enough to stop. 'Are you going to the port?' the driver asked.

'Yes, to the port, for the ferry,' the Manager explained, 'but now we won't be in time.'

'What's up?'

'The distributor.'

'It happened to me a while ago, in February, and I was stuck in the snow, half a metre of snow. Anyway, I've got room for two. Any good? One will have to stay behind.'

'No chance,' said the Manager.

'The three of us are old friends and don't want to be separated,' added the Interrogator.

'Well, goodbye then,' said the driver and left.

There was still one way to avoid the five-kilometre walk to town: the bus. But there wasn't a stop nearby and we had to walk for a quarter of an hour to reach the next one. We stood and waited. We'd taken the luggage, of course, and locked the car.

It was another quarter of an hour before the bus came. A fat lot of use! It was full and the driver waved to show there was no room.

'We're wasting our time,' the Manager complained. 'We'll have to take our suitcases and carry on by foot.'

The Manager was the only one of the three to be at all cheerful. As they walked along, he told jokes or made conversation from time to time to break the melancholy that had descended on the other two, but his efforts were in vain. The Café Sport man said nothing except once when he said that the delay was worst for him: his ordeal wouldn't be over by the evening as he'd expected and he'd have to pass a night of uncertainty. As for the Interrogator, he was more explosive; not ten minutes passed without his cursing and swearing.

'We're nothing but idiots!' he said at one moment. 'Getting stuck because of the distributor just when we were reaching the harbour! It's unbearable!'

'Come on, don't keep complaining,' the Manager told him. 'Bad luck is normal for humankind. Something worse could have happened. A crash or something, or we could have caught fire, or I don't know what.'

'Oh, highly philosophical!'

'I'm just being realistic. Let us say that the journey wasn't just by car and ferry, but by car, ferry, and by foot, and leave it at that.'

At the petrol station at kilometre 217, two kilometres from town, there was a telephone box to the right of the entrance. The pump attendant, a young chap with red hair and covered in freckles, watched them arrive and made a face when they immediately asked for change for the phone.

'We'd better all get in the box,' said the Manager. 'I think there's room. We'll be a bit crowded but never mind.'

We left our cases outside and squeezed into the space, one metre by one and a half.

'Who's going to have the honour of talking to the Chief and telling him the news?' asked the Interrogator.

'It makes no difference; one of us two.'

'Since it makes no difference, I grant you the privilege, manager as you are.'

The Chief wasn't in his office. They told the Manager to wait and not ring off.

It was horribly hot in the phone box, and there was a wasp caught inside, buzzing about, and they wondered which of the three it would choose to sting.

'What's happened? Who is it?' came the Chief's voice loud and clear.

'It's me, the Manager.'

'So? you can't have reached the capital yet. Don't tell me he's got away!'

'No, he's right here beside us; we're all three in the phone box. We're two kilometres from the harbour and we've missed the ferry. The distributor packed up at the 214-kilometre mark on National Route 40.'

The Chief was silent. *Now there'll be an explosion!* thought the Interrogator.

'And what the hell are we going to tell Central? They're expecting you for sure by this evening. I'll have to ring them with the news.'

'What can I say? It was just bad luck; something we couldn't have foreseen.'

'Where exactly are you now?'

'As I said, two kilometres from town, at the 217 post. In a petrol station. Our man's with us here in the phone box. I'm repeating all that so that you can be sure.'

'And what do you plan to do now?'

'We'll look for a repair shop to fix the car, and then we'll leave on the morning ferry at 6.30. Unless you order otherwise.'

'No.'

'Meanwhile what shall we do about our man, until the repair's done, I mean? I say we leave him with the local Special Branch.'

'Out of the question!' said the Chief curtly. 'You hear me? You both hear me? Out of the question! Neither the local Special Branch nor the police must be the slightest bit mixed up in Operation Café Sport. I have strict orders from Central that the affair must be kept between us and them.'

'Very well. But we can't carry him about with us to and from the repair shop. We have to put him *somewhere*.'

'Where you're staying yourselves: at the hotel. Find a room with three beds, not on the ground floor in case he jumps out of the window. Got that? Oh, and with its own bathroom, exclusively its own. That's essential.'

'Agreed. Its own bathroom. I hope we can find one.'

'Of course you can! There are lots of hotels there. Find the best room from the perspective of security and phone me when you've got it arranged.'

'Who should stay with our man and who should go to the repair shop?'

'Either one of you. Not my affair.'

The Chief rang off and we got out of the box.

'He wasn't entirely pleased with the news,' said the Manager.

'What did you expect? That he'd be enthusiastic and congratulate us? Anyway, who's going to the repair shop? Let's agree that now.'

'The repair shop and the actual repair will be a lot of fuss. Obviously both of us would prefer to settle into the hotel.'

'So let's draw lots.'

The Interrogator bent down and gathered some pebbles from the flower-bed on his right, put his hands behind his back, then held out his right fist, 'Odd or even?'

The Manager stood thinking a bit then suddenly decided, 'Odd!'

'You lose. There are four, so I'll stay with our man, and you'll sort out the repair shop and so on.'

'I can't argue, I played and lost... but first let's get to the town and find a hotel. A room with three beds, not on the ground floor, and with its own bathroom.'

It had been years since I'd walked that far. Five whole kilometres. For the journey from home to Special Branch and back I have my car—a little sports car—and what with interrogations one on top of the other I don't have the time or the inclination for walking. The only walking I do is pacing to and fro in my office when some person I'm interrogating is being difficult. It's become a habit— you might say a nervous one—to pace round his chair, as if I wanted to make him dizzy or am looking for a way to solve the mystery.

Well, exhausted, crumpled up, and soaked in sweat from that unexpected midday walk and the stifling heat, we finally reached Station Square. Coming into the town on National Route 40, the first central place one reaches is the railway station, and from its size and appearance, with tall trees, mostly eucalyptus and pepper-trees, and the two fountains, one might expect it to be called 'Railway Station Square' or just 'Station Square' or at least something with 'station' in it, but its official name is something else I can't remember now.

'I'm afraid we'll have some trouble finding the kind of room we want,' said the Manager, 'with three beds, not on the ground floor, and above all with its own bathroom.'

'You think we'll have bad luck here, too?'

'What can I say? I know the hotels are full at this time of year and you can't find a room without a reservation made long in advance.'

'Well then, instead of all three of us running around with our suitcases, better that one goes looking for the room while the others wait.'

'OK', the Manager agreed with my suggestion. 'You wait then, and I'll go from hotel to hotel. Unless we chance on a room at once.'

The two of us went and sat on a bench in about the middle of the square. I had the two cases to my right on the bench, until ten minutes later, when some bad tempered looking chap came along and I put them on the ground to make room.

The square was very busy, with travellers who'd just arrived, and travellers who were running to catch the train at—as always—the last minute; taxis braking and unloading passengers and baggage; shouts, goodbyes, crowds, altogether a lively scene.

In the half-circle of the square there were five hotels in all, and who knows how many more in the side streets.

'I hope we'll find the room we need,' I said to him. 'There are so many hotels round us we'd have to be really unlucky not to get a room.'

'It depends. I don't think it's a matter of good or bad luck. The room we want must have certain features, so the matter is rather whether there is or isn't a room with those features.'

A small boy was going around the benches with combs spread out like a fan in his hand. I called him over and bought one; I'd forgotten my own at home, leaving so early in the morning.

'We must look presentable!' I said as I combed my hair.

I saw him smile. Then he bent down and took up a pebble and juggled it in his hand, before leaning down and putting it carefully on the ground.

'The Manager's taking a long time,' I complained.

Right then we saw him come out of the first hotel he'd tried, the Modern, and he made a gesture with both hands whose meaning wasn't difficult to guess.

'First attempt, zero result,' I said, interpreting it.

'There are another four hotels in the square. He might find a room in one of them.'

'I could do with a cold drink. With this heat, and the walking we did, the nerve-racking breakdown just when all was going well, I don't know, somehow I feel bad.'

'Shall we go over the road? There's a bar there on the right, at the corner.'

'No, the Manager might come out looking for us.'

Actually, we didn't wait long for the Manager to appear again. When he came out of the Station Hotel he made the same gesture with his hands.

The third hotel we saw him go into was the Grand National. He spent longer there. Finally, we saw him coming towards us, beckoning to show that all was well.

'At last I've found a room,' he said. 'I'd begun to lose hope. It doesn't have three beds, only two, but that's easily put right, they'll put a third bed in at once. They told me there's plenty of room for it. And the rest is just as we wanted it: not on the ground floor—it's on the seventh, the top—and with its own bathroom.'

'So all we have to do is go over at once,' I said. 'I've got an awful thirst and I'm desperate for a cold drink.'

The Manager took one suitcase. I went to pick up the other, but our man anticipated me, 'Allow me!'

'Why not?'

'Your room is number 717, and it's ready now,' the receptionist told them. 'We've put in the third bed and I think everything's in order.'

'So we can go up?' asked the Interrogator.

'Certainly you can, only we haven't changed the sheets yet. You're lucky you got the room; I told the gentleman who came in before that the room had only been vacated a quarter of an hour earlier.'

'Don't worry about the sheets,' the Manager told him. 'We're not going to lie down just yet.'

'In any case the maid is going up to make the beds.'

'Tell me, does the room have a telephone?' asked the Interrogator.

The receptionist, seeming offended, turned and answered, 'In the Grand National, sir, all the rooms have telephones. The hotel has an exchange with no fewer than eight—yes, eight—lines!'

'Such perfection!' said the Manager. 'If you could just send three well-chilled orangeades up to the room, that would be ideal.'

'Why don't you ask us what we want?' said the Interrogator. 'We might not want orangeade.'

'Well, orangeade for me,' said the Café Sport man, 'and if it's non-fizzy, so much the better.'

'Excellent. One still and two fizzy,' said the receptionist.

Room 717 didn't have much light but it was spacious. There was just one window, looking onto the inner courtyard which was paved with light beige slabs. From the window there was a ledge which went all along the wall as far as the fire escape stairs, which led straight to the street.

When the three of them went into 717, the Manager and the Interrogator made a quick but careful inspection, while the Café Sport man stood in a corner to the right of the door and then bent to tie his right shoelace, which had come undone once again. He felt dizzy as he straightened up again, and leant against the wall. *I must get my blood pressure measured when I get back from the capital,* he thought.

As for the two Special Branch men, they stopped at the open window and it was obvious they were considering the ledge, twenty-five centimetres wide, wondering if it would be possible for someone to get away on such a narrow ledge, and seven floors up, too. Then they left the window and went into the bathroom. The door to the bathroom didn't have a lock. There was a microscopic window to give light, but not even a cat could get through it, and the Manager said so, 'Not even a cat.'

Meanwhile, the orangeades arrived. The maid brought them—an auburn-haired, very sexy girl. No more than seventeen or eighteen.

'I thought I'd bring the drinks myself since I was coming to make the beds,' and with plenty of wiggling about, she put the orangeades on the little table in front of the window and started to make the beds. She changed the sheets and pillowcases. As she bent down, he could see her breasts—two little circles.

Now the Manager and the Interrogator were over by the door, talking; he couldn't make out what about. The girl went over to the other side of the bed, bent down, and again he saw her breasts—two little circles. He thought, *She'll be in agony. She didn't see me at seven at the post office, she didn't find me at home: how could she guess what's happened to me?* Then, for all that he tried not to look at the girl's breasts a third time, he couldn't resist. But he noticed that her dress was grubby round the armpits, probably from sweat, and he was disgusted.

The Manager passed around the drinks.

'If you want me for anything, I'm always at your disposal,' said the maid as she was leaving.

'I think she meant something by that,' remarked the Interrogator.

'Gentlemen, it is with the profoundest regret that I am obliged to forsake your company,' said the Manager, 'but I really can't delay a second longer,' and he drank his orangeade in one gulp, spilling some on the floor in his haste.

'What are we waiting for?' I asked, breaking the silence. 'Me stuck in this chair and you pacing the room to and fro.'

He was standing in front of the bedside cabinet between his bed and mine, struggling to open the drawer, which was stuck.

'We're waiting for the Manager to phone us,' he told me and with one more heave he got the drawer open. 'As if you didn't know it. He's been gone twenty minutes; looks as if he hasn't worked out which repair shop will fix the thing.'

'Yes, he should be ringing us any minute. You know, doing nothing for so long and the silence that's fallen on us has got on my nerves. What d'you think? Shall we play something to pass the time? Cards? Chess?'

'Not cards, I don't play. I was obsessed with them once, but it's been three years now that I've given them up completely. As for chess, fine. D'you think the hotel's got a set?'

'Probably. If not, we could ask them to borrow a set from one of the cafés round here.'

I called reception on the phone and they told me the hotel would bring us a set. In a little while we'd set up a game. Oh yes, I played black.

Just when the first game was over—he got checkmate on the sixth move—the phone rang.

'The Manager!' I exclaimed and picked up the receiver. 'Tell us, then! What's happening? Repair shop OK?'

'What repair shop, what are you talking about?' came an angry woman's voice, piercing and with a strange tone to it.

'What do you want, madam?'

'What do *you* want?'

'For you to leave me alone! What number did you want?'

'Isn't that 707?'

'No.'

'Well, what is it then?'

I rang off and put a stop to her nonsense.

'I thought it was the Manager,' he said.

'It doesn't matter. He'll be looking for a repair shop. I'm sure he'll phone shortly.'

He started the second game with a really good opening.

'I must admit I didn't expect you to play so well,' I told him.

'And you should know that I haven't played for the last four or five years. I don't play regularly.'

'If we carry on like this I'm not going to win a single game.'

I thought a bit, then played a knight.

'Where's this leading?' He frowned. 'You've got something in mind.'

'Or maybe I haven't and I played it by chance.'

The phone rang. 'Manager here,' came the voice before I'd hardly picked it up. 'I'm at the workshop and I'm phoning as I said I would. We're about to go and tow the car in. When we're back, I'll ring again and tell you the details.'

'OK, we're fine; we're playing chess. What the hell's making that noise?'

'That noise? Isn't it obvious? This is a car repair shop, not a clinic with signs demanding "Silence".'

'I've played!' he said and scratched the scar below his ear with his middle finger.

'Hmm! You put me in a difficult position. That mad move you made looks very dangerous.'

'Not at all! It'll be very difficult for me to save the game. The situation gets worse move by move.'

'I think you're exaggerating,' said the Interrogator. 'Why such pessimism?'

'Whatever you say, I won't change my opinion. There's an eighty percent chance the game's lost. I don't see any way out of it; my men are bleeding away.'

With the air of a specialist ready to give his diagnosis, the Interrogator said, 'I have to admit your situation is quite difficult, but no more than that. Anyway, as you know, in chess as in love it's no use prognosticating. A game of chess or a game of love is lost or won at the last moment.'

He half-smiled at the comparison. 'As for love, yes, I agree. But not for chess. In the end, I think the best I can do is launch another attack, using all my might.'

The Interrogator responded with enthusiasm, 'Bravo! A heroic decision worthy of our congratulations!'

And as if to underline his approval, he took the right-hand rook—it was his turn to play—and moved it, banging it down on the board.

'And now, counterattack!' he replied in kind, immediately following the Interrogator's move.

He made his counterattack with his one remaining knight.

The Interrogator frowned, 'This needs care. The enemy is trying desperately first to save himself and then to turn the tables. But I shall treat him appropriately. He won't catch me napping!'

'I'm delighted by your confidence and I'm waiting for the result,' he said, taking out his cigarette packet. 'Cigarette?'

The Interrogator looked at him as if he hadn't understood, then took one. 'I accept with pleasure, even though your brand is rather strong for me. Let me see —yes, this pawn here could take a step forward; why not?'

In the end, the Interrogator won the game.

'I told you before,' said the other, 'I didn't stand a chance. It was obvious.'

'Now I've won a game, things are happening! We're three to one. Shall we go on?'

'Why not?'

'Another suggestion: let's drink something refreshing; this heat calls for it.'

'I wouldn't mind. I'd be glad of an orangeade.'

'Fine! A fizzy one for me and a still one for you.'

He picked up the phone and asked for the bar.

They'd already started on a new game when there was a knock at the door.

'The orangeades!' said the Interrogator. 'Slow service; let's hope that at least they'll be well chilled.'

He got up and looked for the key. He thought it was in his jacket, but finally found it in his right-hand trouser pocket.

The maid came in, the one who'd made the beds; she swung her hips even more. 'I brought the drinks myself,' she said, 'because the barman was busy; these young men are completely indifferent. Personally, I prefer mature men.'

She put the orangeades on the little table, which she brought up close to where they were playing, and with the tray in her hand she stood over them. 'How I like that game!' she said, fiddling with her hair.

'It's not as difficult as it looks,' said the Interrogator.

'Really? Tell me, do you plan to stay long in our hotel?'

'Well, it depends. Yes and no, according to how our business goes.'

'I wish I could learn to play chess, find a gentleman to teach me. How I like it! And in general I like all games; I'm crazy about games,' and she smiled of suggestively.

'We must get back to our game,' said the Interrogator curtly. They took their places, ready to continue.

The girl waited a little, then, annoyed that they didn't take any notice of her, decided to make for the door, with less hip-swinging now.

He waited for her to get down the corridor, and decided she was far enough away not to hear the key before he got up and double-bolted the door.

They became immersed in the game—the sixth round had started a little while before. So far, the score was three games to the Café Sport man and two to the Interrogator.

'Either we'll come out equal with this game or it'll be four to two,' said the Interrogator, playing a pawn.

'If I keep my cool, I think I'll beat you a fourth time.'

'What does "If I keep my cool" mean? As far as I can see you're exceptionally calm; I don't understand.'

'No, I'm not completely calm. I'm under pressure to beat you, and it makes me rush.'

'You don't seem to me to be rushing. You're a maestro! You could teach lots of people.'

'Including the maid?'

The Interrogator, who had been about to move one of his knights, stopped, 'You mean she made an impression on you?'

'A tasty little thing, I agree. But when she lifted up her hand to fix her hair I could see her bra under the armpit and it was dirty. Probably sweat, and it made me sick. I can't bear a woman whose underwear isn't spotless.'

'As to that, our tastes agree,' said the Interrogator and moved his knight to the right.

The phone rang. 'The Manager again!' he shouted picking it up. 'Tell us! What's the news? What about the distributor?'

'Not so good.'

'Meaning?'

'We're stuck! The business is going to take us all night. They had to fix some other cars, and then we found it wasn't just the distributor. The valves have got to be adjusted, the clutch relined, etc., etc.'

'Oh no.'

Mixed up with the Manager's voice there came the noise of the workshop.

'Well, I've got nothing else to tell you,' the Manager said as if he were in a hurry. 'As soon as the car's fixed I'll take it and come to the Grand National and we'll go straight to the ferry because it doesn't look as if they'll finish before five in the morning.'

'OK, what can I say? The way things are, there's no use talking about it. But we'll have to tell the Chief. You ring him up, like before, yes?'

Horribly irritated, the Interrogator clenched his left fist and thumped the little table, upsetting the glasses.

'I tell you the business will take all night,' the Manager continued, 'There's nothing to be done!'

'Damn it to hell!'

'I said that myself, and not just once.'

'So, what happens now?'

'What do you expect to happen? I'll stay at the repair shop. Unless I'm leaning over them, following the job, we won't even get done by tomorrow. As for you, what can I say? Do whatever you think best.'

That was the end of the conversation. The Interrogator, beside himself, went to the closed window and looked out, then he went to the door, then back to the window and opened it and stood in front of it.

'Very fine weather,' he said, 'And very fine what the Manager said. The job will take all night!'

Leaving the window open, he returned to the chess match.

'Whose move?' he asked.

'Yours.'

'I'll play standing up. You don't mind?'

'No, why should I mind?'

'I can't possibly sit down; I'm so annoyed I just can't be glued to a chair.'

No more than three minutes later the game was broken off again, this time by the Interrogator.

'I'm not in the mood' he said suddenly, kicking the chair beside him.

'I understand your frustration. I want you to believe...'

'And I want to go to the toilet!' he interrupted. 'You come, too, and stand outside the door. I'm not at all inclined for you to make any trouble for me!'

They got up and the Interrogator went towards the toilet, but halfway there he turned and closed the window. Then he went into the bathroom while the other stood by the half-open door.

'Not like that!' the Interrogator called. 'Talk, say something, anything, but loud so I can hear you, so I know you're there all the time.'

'What shall I say?'

'Can't you think of anything? The national anthem.'

'Shall I sing it?'

'Yes, sing it.'

'I sing very out of tune.'

'It doesn't matter, you're not giving a recital. Come on, sing so I can hear you!'

He started the national anthem but stopped at the third verse; he couldn't remember any more so he went back to the first.

'Stop! I've got an idea, a fantastic idea!'

'And it came to you in the toilet?'

'Yes, my best ideas always come to me like that, in the toilet.'

'So, what's your idea?'

'A walk round the town!' called the Interrogator loudly, and flushed the toilet. 'How does that sound to you?'

'Well, I find your idea... first class.'

The Interrogator laughed. 'I expected you to say it was very suspicious.'

'Suspicious? Why?'

'Well, it's such a good idea that it seems very strange, suspicious. But it's quite simple what I suggest. Notice, it's a suggestion, nothing more. If you agree with my suggestion, that's fine, we'll really take a stroll round the town. If not, the suggestion is cancelled and we won't go.'

'I agree!'

'Then off we go! I want to explain something first. I feel stifled in here, and since the Manager telephoned and gave me the altogether unwelcome news that the repair's going to take all night, until five in the morning—Ah, no! I can't bear to stay locked up in room 717 of the Grand National for almost twenty-four hours. Besides, I'm responsible for you as long as we're together. Just me! And I believe you wouldn't dare, under any circumstances, to play an ugly trick on me.'

'There's no question of my playing any tricks.'

'At least, I should inform you that I've won first prize four times for marksmanship with a pistol. And you wouldn't get far if you wanted to...'

'I don't want any such thing!' he said curtly.

'Fine! I won't return to the subject, I've said what I had to. But I should add that we'll follow my idea only if you agree. A stroll by force is no good! And I can't put handcuffs on you and pull you around tied up.'

'Why are you going on about it? If I didn't fancy the idea, I would have told you at once. I've heard your idea, and I have no objection to it.'

The Interrogator stubbed out his cigarette and said, 'One hour long; we'll time it. I think one hour's right.'

'I agree to one hour, too.'

'Fine! The first thing we've got to do is get out of here,' he said, unlocking the door. 'And the second is a good shave; it'll freshen up the pair of us.'

'What would you say to a really close shave?' he asked, bending close to me with an air as if he'd said, 'How about a joint?' or 'Fancy a Lolita type?'

The way he was leaning over me I could feel his hot breath on the nape of my neck. Damp and hot, like those steamy towels which in a little while, when the shaving was finished, he'd stick on my face to take away the burning.

It made my hair stand on end to feel his breath suddenly creeping over me. Nauseating!

In a green plastic cup on the edge of the basin there were some mint leaves, and all the time he was shaving me he'd take a leaf and chew it. Then, when he'd got all the juice out, he'd spit it out hard, vengefully one might say, onto the mosaic floor, and immediately take another leaf.

Well, I've never been able to stand mint. I've got an allergy. And in these circumstances a double allergy, being face-to-face not just with the mint but with the green plastic cup garnished with shaving foam, half dried up, too, like stale whipped cream or an old man's spit left on his chin unwiped and drying out, because he kept picking up the cup with fingers covered in foam.

'Any thoughts about that extra-close shave?' he asked again. 'Did you decide?'

I could have sent him straight to hell with his really close shave, but I decided not to.

'OK,' I said unenthusiastically to make an end of it, 'since you insist and force me to it.'

'Wonderful!' He positively melted with enthusiasm as if I'd announced I don't know what.

And with almost dance-like movements—not almost, but completely dance-like—he started to sharpen his razor again.

'Be careful, eh?' I said, 'You see I have very sensitive skin. At the first nick it tears like cigarette paper and bleeds, and I don't like blood at all!'

He smiled. A twisted sort of smile, and I saw a bit of mint leaf stuck on one of his lower teeth and it turned me up.

'Ah, don't worry,' he said, as if telling me off and comforting me at the same time, 'I have a very light hand, I do. And if you didn't know it, you'll find out that close shaves are my speciality.'

'Oh yes?' I said, feigning great interest. 'Is that so? I wouldn't have known it, I confess to a lack of that knowledge. But in that case, everything's going to be fine.'

He kept sharpening his razor and murmuring a song every now and then. I couldn't have said what song. And anyway, I didn't care.

'It's very hot!' he remarked as if I were somehow responsible.

'Hot? Ah, yes, it's hot... very hot.'

He looked at me strangely. '"Very" isn't the word,' he insisted. 'It's fearfully hot.'

'OK, just as you like. Cross out "very" and put "fearfully."'

He was quiet then for two or three minutes and I kidded myself his battery had run out, but no such luck.

'You know something,' he whispered conspiratorially, again, 'that jacket... why don't you take off your jacket and get some relief?'

I threw him a glance as if he were a moron.

'You know what?' I told him as soon as I'd recovered. 'No, I don't plan to take my jacket off. I can't be bothered. You understand? I'm fed up with taking off and putting on. Our close shave's nearly over anyway.'

'Ah, no!' he chirruped. 'Close shaves have their rules. Please don't rush me. Above all, don't rush me.'

I didn't reply. He'd just about driven me mad me with his chatter. The only thing I could do was to take no notice of him and offer no pretext for conversation; what else?

Very optimistic, or rather naïve. In less than thirty seconds he started again.

'This heat! It's driving me mad!'

He unbuttoned the top two buttons of his shirt—he didn't have a tie on and his collar was open. Some long strawberry-blond, sweaty hairs popped out. Oh, yes; he had a medallion on his chest. Gold? Maybe. I looked to see what was on it, but couldn't make it out. At first I thought it was two doves, then I thought no, not doves, chickens.

'Your friend's more practical!' The razor-man, now at work on my right cheek, carried on fiddling his tune. 'Did you see? he's taken his jacket off and relaxed... you, however... you're stubborn!'

What could I say now? Sit there and tell him the details of the matter? That it was out of the question for me to take my jacket off, even if I melted from the heat. Not because I didn't want to; of course I knew how hot it was. No, it was because of my 'friend' who was sitting quietly leafing through an illustrated magazine on the table waiting his turn for a shave... Well, should my 'friend' take it into his head to make a neat move for the exit at some moment, then I would be obliged to pull out my pistol. And since I had my pistol in my jacket, in the middle pocket on the left...

Well, if I were to sit down and give him all these explanations, there's no doubt he would sympathise. But it was out of the question to tell him. So I had to let him witter on about my jacket until he was finally exhausted.

When the two of us had gone into the barber's, which was called 'Sincerity', all four chairs had been taken. We were undecided; should we stay? Go elsewhere? Just then one of the chairs was vacated, the first one on the right. The man with the razor, who had something in his mouth and was chewing—I didn't know yet that it was mint, if I had we'd have left at once—looked at me enquiringly. 'Which of the two gentlemen will go first?' he asked me. 'You or your friend?'

I decided to go first.

Of course, all the time I was in the barber's chair I watched our man closely in the mirror that took up all the wall. I didn't miss his slightest movement or change of expression on his face or in his eyes. For the moment, at least, nothing suspicious. Seated at the little oval table at the far end of the shop, he leafed through the magazines there, and smoked from time to time—no, he smoked a lot, more than usual—he gazed at the street, Veterans Avenue, absent-mindedly. Absent-mindedly?

Twice he played with the shop cat, which was frisking about near him. First he stroked it with the back of his hand, and the cat lay on its back. Then he stroked and pulled its whiskers, and the cat was understandably annoyed. As for his jacket, he'd thrown it carelessly onto the chair nearby. Nothing suspicious, as I think I said before. But how could I be one hundred percent sure? Perhaps he had some plan in mind, a plan to get away from me? At some given moment to dash for the exit, to slip like quicksilver through the half-open door and mingle with the crowd on Veterans Avenue, to disappear in it? I certainly had no guarantee he wasn't cooking up some such plan. The only thing I could do was exactly what I was doing: not stop for a moment my systematic surveillance of him in the mirror.

'This heat's killing me!' the man with the razor complained again, and he undid a fourth and a fifth button. Then he put his hand, still with some foam on it, into the opening and scratched himself, right down to the belly button, maybe further.

'Indeed,' I said, 'your town is very hot.'

Why did I speak? Like a fool I'd fed his idle chatter.

'Our town!' he said. 'That's to say, you're not from here?'

I shook my head.

'Neither you nor your friend?'

Again I shook my head.

'So how do you come to be in our town? Business?'

I nodded.

'What kind of business?'

It was impossible to escape.

'We're travelling salesmen,' I said.

'Travelling salesmen!' He burst out as if he'd heard something incredible such as 'a pilot of supersonic aeroplanes' or 'a lion tamer'.

'You find that strange?' I asked him.

'No, just very charming,' he said and made a movement with his hand in the air as if chasing away butterflies. 'You know, it was always my dream to be a travelling salesman. In the end, I just became a barber. If I weren't a barber I'd like to be a salesman. A travelling salesman.'

'Very interesting. But don't give up hope: in life, it's never too late.'

'Ah, you give me some hope!' he said and made his butterfly-chasing movement again. 'I'm very glad that we have basically the same tastes.'

'Ah, no!' I interrupted, terrorised by his dancing movements, 'I find that a bit much, don't you think?'

'And what exactly do you sell?'

I don't know why, but at that moment Operation Toilet Paper came to my mind. 'Toilet paper,' I said.

'Ooh!' he said, shocked.

'A basic necessity!' I continued just to upset him, and in tones as if I were announcing a public holiday, 'Toilet paper is one of the foundations of civilised society, one of the...'

'Fine, but let's leave the subject,' he interrupted. 'Tell me, what about your jacket, are you going to take it off after all, yes or no?'

I gestured to him to bend closer.

'Listen, I'll tell you what it is,' I whispered very con-
fidentially. 'In the inside left pocket of my jacket I happen
to have a pistol. Oh, only a tiny one, but I might suddenly
need it, you understand?'

'I understand that you're pulling my leg,' he said in a
disappointed tone as if I'd insulted him.

That way I finally got some peace from the man with
the razor and his talk. But not from the fly, a horrible
bluebottle that came and settled sometimes on my left
cheek, sometimes on my right, to taste the shaving foam.
I lifted my hand to chase it away. Then I caught sight
of him in the mirror looking at me, making out that he
wasn't, peeping from behind a Sunday colour supple-
ment. At the exact same moment, the same second I
lifted my hand, he looked at me. So, he was spying on
me while pretending to look at the magazine! This seriously raised my suspicions. He was probably thinking
up something cunning! For the moment I didn't show
any uneasiness, or even indicate that I'd seen him looking
at me, but I put myself 'on guard', so to speak. For all
that I didn't show anything, I couldn't resist smiling at
the thought of what might happen in the elegant, re-
spectable barber's shop if my 'friend' made a dash for
the way out, with me behind him with the towel tied
round my neck, one cheek covered in foam and the pistol in my hand.

Freshly shaved, we stood for a moment or two on the pavement outside 'Sincerity'. Not in front of the entrance; a touch to the right.

The midday sun, strong as it was, hurt our eyes. We weren't used to bright light after all the time we were in the barber's chairs. They had had the blinds drawn, so that the unbearably bright September sun reached us transformed into a gentle light.

'You have a little blood on your scar,' I told him, 'below your ear.'

'Oh yes? I didn't notice it was bleeding.' He wiped it off carefully with his finger.

'It seems he didn't notice he'd cut you; how would he, with all his silly chatter!'

He explained that the scar was especially sensitive and bled easily. 'It's a good job I have excellent blood,' he added. 'It stops at once, sets, and it's never got infected.'

'That's all very interesting. And now to business: a stroll around the town. We decided on an hour.'

He looked at me. 'Not a whole hour,' he remarked. 'Minus the twenty minutes for shaving.'

'No, I am not the kind to cheat. Our stroll starts now. It's 2.05, so we have until 3.05.'

He looked very pleased. 'So much the better!' he said. 'Well, shall we start?'

'Wait, what do you mean "start"? Have you got anything special to suggest? Where do you think we should go?'

'I can't think of any place. Anyway, I don't know the town well. What am I saying? It's practically unknown to me. I passed through it three times, years ago, and in a hurry.'

So I made the first move, suggesting we stroll randomly. 'I think that's the best idea,' I added. 'To go wherever the road takes us. To drift with the town's movements, as if we were at sea drifting with the current.'

'Bravo!' he said. 'I like the way you think. A walk at random... fine! I have a taste for following chance. I go for the unplanned, the unexpected.'

'Agreed. I, too, don't know the town one hundred percent, though I've wandered in it before.'

The barber's shop was at 115 Veterans Avenue. We started by going down towards number one, towards the town centre.

We went at our own pace; we had no reason to hurry. The traffic grew heavier and heavier. Light at first, it would reach its peak in the evening.

I was on the left, he on the right. What exactly did we do? A lot, and nothing. Whatever two people who've gone out for a walk in the town do when they have no plans, no errands.

We gazed in the shop windows. From time to time we stopped and looked at something that attracted our attention, or lingered without reason in front of unlikely windows, for example women's hats or ironmongery. We would examine the display in the window and listen to the remarks of others who'd stopped beside us, giving our own opinions, too. About a woman's hat with multi-coloured feathers and a whole bird in the middle I said, 'Amazing! Just the thing for the big carnival parade,' and he agreed, 'I'm sure it would get the prize for eccentricity.'

In general, our wanderings had a very relaxed rhythm; wandering just for the sake of it, no aim or programme.

Why bother to say exactly which roads we went along, where exactly we stopped, what we said, word for word? We didn't reach the end of Veterans Avenue; somewhere further down we turned left onto Acacia Avenue. Then we crossed Popular Theatre Square and went into—I don't remember or didn't notice which avenue. From there we went onto less central roads—and at one point we found ourselves on Veterans Avenue again, somewhere around number fifty-five or fifty-seven, and carried on to number one.

It's not as if we didn't talk as we walked; when we weren't in front of a window looking at a strange hat or something, we chatted continually. On various subjects: sometimes about a girl who caught our attention, sometimes about a film.

We'd done about half an hour's walking when we reached the crossing of Veterans Avenue with Triumph Avenue, one of the most central points in the city. Here we stopped for some time, about ten minutes, because there was an accident involving a bus and a taxi that had attracted much curiosity. We got closer ourselves and followed the argument between the two drivers. It hadn't got further than an exchange of civilities, but things were about to develop more seriously when a policeman appeared. It's usual in such cases that a policeman arrives at a vital moment and spoils the fun. The bystanders, including the two of us, weren't ready to move on, and it needed the arrival of a second policeman before we obeyed the order to go about our own business.

Bit by bit, as we went along, the atmosphere between us warmed up. Not a lot, not too much and not suddenly, but it was clear that there was some warmth between us. Nothing remarkable in that, just that our walk changed in the character it had begun with and became more relaxed and friendly. And this was particularly apparent when we got onto the subject that two men always talk about when they go for a walk together: women.

In University Square we stopped at the kiosk by Triumph Avenue. He wanted to get some cigarettes. There, just as we were standing in front of the kiosk as he paid for his cigarettes, I at last saw the other agent, maybe twenty metres away, standing in front of a window and pretending to be interested in its contents.

'Gentlemen, it is with the profoundest regret that I am obliged to forsake your company!' said the Manager in the style of one making a speech at an important gathering. 'But it is impossible to delay any longer, by not even for so much as a second!'

And he drank his orangeade in one gulp, spilling some onto the floor in his hurry.

'I am eternally careless! If I haven't got a steering wheel or a pistol in my hands, they shake as if I've got Parkinson's. Anyway, please excuse me!'

He mopped up the sweat that had gathered on his face and neck with his handkerchief, stepped over the spilt orangeade, and opened the door.

'You'd better call the Chief yourself,' the Interrogator told him. 'It wouldn't do to phone from here via the hotel exchange and let them know we're Special Branch.'

'OK, I'll call from a box and tell him we found a room in the Grand National. And now, off I go! I'll find a workshop, get the car towed in and see what the hell's wrong with the distributor... I'll ring from whichever workshop I end up in. What a pain! If only I'd chosen evens instead of odds. Then I'd be sitting calmly in my room in the Grand National instead of running around in the heat struggling with the distributor and everything. You escaped all that, lucky sod!'

And he dashed into the corridor with such force that he'd have tripped over the barman with his tray full of drinks, if he'd happened to be passing in the corridor outside room 717 just then. But, in fact, not only was the barman not passing, but the Manager, as soon as he'd closed the door behind him, seemed to lose speed and energy and walked at his own gentle pace towards the lifts at the end of the corridor. He even stopped halfway to gaze curiously at a strange plant in a pot. Some sort of cactus.

At a gentle pace he continued to the lifts. He waited patiently to get one of the two. They were continually engaged. He waited at least five minutes if not more. In other circumstances he'd have raged at the delay like a wild beast and taken the stairs so as not to be late, but this time he wasn't at all concerned. He wasn't even annoyed with the woman who got in at the fourth floor wearing such strong perfume it gassed out the little space of the lift.

Calmly, he crossed the boundless hall of the Grand National, went out onto the pavement, bought cigarettes at the kiosk on the corner, then crossed to the opposite pavement where the bar The Six Fingers had its entrance exactly opposite the hotel's. Anyone sitting at a table behind the big window of the bar and looking over to the Grand National would have complete oversight of who went in or came out.

The Manager didn't go to the back of the barroom. He went and stood beside a table in the corner, right up against the big window, where someone was drinking tomato juice and reading the *Town Chronicle,* one of the town's two evening papers. The other was the *Evening News.* Without a word, the Manager drew up a chair and sat down.

'I want to drink something!' he called to the waiter, who was standing about with two others and showing total indifference to the new customer.

'What would the gentleman like?' said the waiter without moving and clearly annoyed by the interruption.

'What would I like? Well, a brandy. Make it a double.'

The person with the tomato juice leant over and said, 'Now that you've asked for a double brandy, all you have to do is ask for a black pencil and take the paper from your cigarette packet and draw two little circles.'

The Manager laughed aloud, 'Oh, come on, this isn't the Café Sport.'

'What news? All OK?'

'OK.'

'Tell me already! I'm bored with waiting. I've been here an hour and a half drinking endless tomato juices. I just had to tell myself to hang on, I thought all these tomato juices would keep making me go to the toilet, and that wouldn't do.'

'I sympathise. When you have to keep an eye out, it wouldn't do to keep going off to the toilet every five minutes.'

The waiter brought the double brandy, spilling some on the way.

'I'm listening!' said the other to the Manager.

'Don't be in such a hurry! Let me have a sip of my drink first and then I'll tell you everything in detail. Now that I'm off duty until five o'clock tomorrow morning and free to drink alcohol, instead of orangeade, which I was drinking just now, or tomato juice…'

'You can do what you like and drink what you like. Brandy? Brandy. As for me, no! Strictly forbidden to touch alcohol until I go off duty. You know, I came much earlier than the planned hour. As I said, I've been here in the Six Fingers an hour and a half. I opened up on the road and reached 130.'

'We went at 110. It would have been easy to do 130 or even 140, but, you know, the Chief planned for 110 and it wasn't on to do more. We were bound to be at the 214-kilometre marker at the time arranged, regular as clockwork.'

'Tell me, did you see me overtaking you just past the junction with National Route 40?'

'As if I didn't notice! That's to say, I recognised the car, and understood. I nearly sent you to hell, the way you came up and stuck to us. If I hadn't swerved left at once we would have crashed. Well, all's going well so far. As for the Interrogator, what can I say? He's an ace!'

'Plays his part well, eh?

'An ace, I tell you! He does it gently, as if nothing's going on. How could the other one guess the scenario?'

'So, the wheels are turning.'

'Superbly!'

'And now, the continuation. Your two telephone calls, then they go out for their walk, and then I come onto the scene.'

'And you start to play theatre, though yours is a non-speaking part.'

'Yes, but my pistol won't be dumb if the need arises.'

'In a word, everything's going like clockwork. Oh, yes, something unforeseen happened on the road; we nearly had it.'

'What happened?'

'Well, when I'd stopped and was pretending to look and see what was wrong with the engine, at kilometre 214 on National Route 40, just as I'd told the others that there was a fault with the distributor, a traffic policeman turned up on his motorbike. An awkward chap, you could see it a mile off. "What's going on here?" he said and got out his book to give us a ticket. He was looking at us suspiciously, too. "It's the distributor," I said, "we're stuck because of the distributor." What luck to find someone so thick! He went over and bent down to look at the engine and my heart was nearly bursting, a pulse of 200 a minute. I managed to exchange glances with the Interrogator and I could see he, too, was frozen with fear. Sure, if we'd told him we were Special Branch, if we'd shown him our yellow identity cards, the moment he saw them he'd have been all apology, but we didn't dare. The Café Sport man was looking out from his corner. He'd have guessed at once that it was all a piece of theatre so we couldn't let the traffic policeman look at the engine himself. Luckily we got away with it at the last minute! They radioed the cop to go to 305 on the National Road where there'd been a crash, so he had to leave us. A last-minute escape!'

'Almost a catastrophe! And all for nothing. How could anyone expect such a thing?'

'The point is we got away with it, and all has gone well for the time being. I hope it will continue that way to the end. I've left them now in room 717. We ordered three orangeades, and I left in a hurry, saying I was going to the repair shop, and in my hurry, I spilt some orangeade on the floor. I did it deliberately, a sudden idea. They must be playing chess now, if our man plays and feels like a game. He may not want to. If they don't play chess, they'll talk about various things, like the weather.

The Interrogator's waiting for my telephone call—the first—which is supposed to be from the repair shop. In fact, it's time I made that call now.'

The other took his glass—nearly half full of tomato juice—and went to drink it, then he left it on the marble table-top without drinking a sip.

'The important moment,' he said as if talking to himself and not to the Manager, 'is the moment the Interrogator suggests a walk in the town. Let's hope our man doesn't refuse. Nothing's out of the question, though. He might be suspicious that we've laid a trap for him—though probably impossible—or he may just not feel like a walk.'

The Manager laughed. 'It's quite good this brandy!' he said, taking another sip or two. 'What can I say? I have complete faith in the Interrogator. You should have seen him, from the moment we started and all during the journey, you should have seen how he handled the operation. Gently, I tell you, all modest and humble.'

'I'm very curious how this Operation Café Sport will turn out.'

The Manager didn't continue the conversation but got up and went to the telephone, to the right of the toilet. There was an old-fashioned electric fan there, making noise as if there were great machines at work.

'The Manager here,' he said to the Interrogator. 'I'm calling you from the workshop, as we agreed. We'll be off soon to tow the car in. When we arrive, I'll phone you again and tell you what condition it's in. That noise? No need to ask! This is a car repair shop, not a clinic with signs demanding "Silence".

After he'd made the call, he returned to his place. 'All's going well,' he said, 'They're playing chess now.'

'What else did he tell you?'

'What else? Oh, yes, the funny thing was he asked me what the noise was that made it so difficult to hear. What a coincidence that the fan next to the telephone made a noise as if machines were at work. Our man, who was probably beside the Interrogator, must have heard the noise and is not in the slightest doubt that I was in the repair shop. Now we'll wait half an hour and then it's time for the second call. Meanwhile I think I'll have another brandy.'

'I shan't be long, ten minutes, fifteen at the very most,' the Chief told us when the head photographer told him about the microfilm—what about the microfilm? That it had been developed and he was waiting for the Chief to come and see them there.

While the Chief was away, the Manager and I stayed in his office—he'd told us not to leave—and I confess I was wildly curious about this Operation Café Sport.

The quarter of an hour became half an hour, then nearly three quarters. It seemed the microfilm was very interesting! At last the door opened and he came rushing in as if he didn't want to lose a second. He tripped on the way in.

'What the hell's happening to me today!' he complained. 'I keep tripping. Well, where were we?'

'At the ferry,' the Manager put in, 'when they interrupted us, you had just told us that you'd already informed the Café Sport man that he was being brought to Central. And that we would leave with a Special Branch car and take the 11.10 ferry, so as to be in the capital the same day.'

I saw the Chief smile and look at us over the top of his glasses, those probably fake glasses, which he wore rather low on his nose.

'Yes, that's what I had in fact told our man. For yourselves, however, I have something special: You're to set out early in the morning, seven o'clock, so as to reach Central in the afternoon, but there's no question of your actually arriving.'

Both of us looked at him in surprise.

'It's very simple,' he continued. 'You won't reach Central in the afternoon because you won't make the ferry. No! At kilometre 214 on the National Route 40, your car will stop. A faulty distributor. Exactly according to plan.'

He went to his desk and searched among some papers, then he picked up the receiver and made as if to dial a number, but didn't do it after all: he just untangled the twisted cable.

'You will be informed of the continuation of the Plan in full detail. And you will ask about any doubts you may have, if you have any. First, I must give some clarification about this interruption to the journey: the other Café Sport man, the one in the photograph, is just as I explained, with one difference: he's no longer alive.'

Unbelievable! This unexpected information so surprised me that I left my nearly finished cigarette in my mouth and burnt my lip. The way the Chief had explained Operation Café Sport until then I couldn't have suspected—not I, nor any third party—that such a circumstance had intervened.

'And now, to give you the facts in the order they occurred. When our man was arrested, two agents followed the other, the one in the photograph. They weren't sure that the man with the double brandy was the one he was in fact planning to meet. Suppose that short conversation they'd had about treading on his foot had no significance and was just chance? Suppose the suspect in the photograph was to make contact not with the man we had already arrested but with some other we had not pinpointed? The two agents let him proceed through the café and go outside. He turned left on Independence Avenue at a normal pace and stopped at the crossing with National Library Street, right by the traffic lights. He stayed there two or three minutes, in spite of the fact that the pedestrian crossing light had come on twice and if he'd wanted to he could have crossed. A suspicious sign! Why didn't he cross at once? What was he waiting for? *Who* was he waiting for? Our agents left him to wait at the lights. Maybe at that point some third man would approach him by prior arrangement. Who was he expecting? The double-brandy man, who, if he hadn't been arrested, would come out of the café to meet him a second time? Or someone else? In the end no-one came and the suspect finally crossed the road and continued directly along Independence Avenue, but at a fast pace now. The agents reached him and walked one to each side of him. They told him to follow them to the Special Branch offices. The strange thing was he didn't seem at all troubled, as if he was already resigned to his fate. He said, 'OK.' Nothing more. They'd hardly gone ten metres, towards the car parked a little further on, when the suspect started to run. Our agents didn't just stand there with their hands in their pockets. At close range they called out to him to stop or they'd fire. He didn't obey but ran faster. Then they shot. They aimed low, at the legs, so that the bullets would merely render him immobile. But at that moment our man lost his footing—something on the pavement, a loose slab, I don't know exactly and it doesn't matter. He bent, practically doubled up onto his knees, and the bullet—just one bullet—got him not on the legs but higher. So much higher that he remained there on the spot, face down on the pavement in front of the Star Cinema.'

'What bad luck!' I said.

'Bad luck for the Special Branch!' corrected the Chief as if I hadn't exactly meant that. 'An irrevocable accident! And worse still, we didn't find anything on him. Not a thing in his pockets, nor in the soles or the heels of his shoes. He had no identification or anything else to give us a lead.'

'So we don't know who he is?' asked the Manager.

The Chief shook his head and continued, 'I don't think it's necessary to tell you that I haven't mentioned the death to the man from the Café Sport. On the contrary, I gave him the impression that his partner in crime was arrested and we're questioning him ceaselessly. Ah, yes, and I told him, too, as if it were incidental, that in the questioning we had uncovered some very interesting information. He took it calmly and asked for the facts. "Of course, there's no question of his being my partner in crime," he said again. I avoided opening up with much conversation. "Soon, as soon as we've finished some additional questioning which we're carrying out now, I shall order that the two of you are brought to my office so that I can question you together." He didn't seem troubled or the slightest bit uneasy. "That's what I should like, too, to be examined face-to-face with him," he said.'

'Did you inform him that we would be taking him to Central tomorrow?' I asked.

'Hold your horses!' the Chief retorted. 'I ought to tell you what I did when I started the interrogation. I had the unfavourable, the especially unfavourable fact that one of the two was no longer in a position to give us any information. On the other hand, his partner in crime—because of course we have to assume from the outset that he is guilty—denies any connection with him. Nothing was found when we searched his house and its environs. Meanwhile I had many telephone conversations with Central. What's the answer? To let him go? No, that solution is out of the question. To interrogate him in a somewhat less subtle and gentle way than hitherto? Miracles could happen with a second interrogation done on a different basis. That's to say, with a different method and under different circumstances. Central however said no. And they gave me orders to set the Plan in motion. I digress here and continue with what happened after I'd communicated with Central. Well, I reminded him that I'd told him half an hour earlier that we would be taking him to the capital tomorrow, to Central. And that the other, his partner in crime, had already been sent there. That's to say, that we'd already sent him to Central on their orders. Of necessity, I told him, he, too, would be sent to Central and the further interrogation would take place there. Still, he seemed calm. "There's no point in giving me all this trouble, there's no question of your finding anything out," he said. Here ends my direct personal involvement with the Café Sport man. They took him to his room, and they've just told me, now, when I went to the photographer, that he's pacing from wall to wall and smoking continually. They follow his movements through a supposed picture on the wall.'

'I'm impatient to hear about the Plan,' said the Manager.

'The Plan is Central's own creation. Who invented it, I don't know. Maybe it's the result, the fruit, of a combined effort. I don't know who is or are the inventors of the Plan or even if it was an electronic brain. What I'm not ignorant of, in fact I know it very well, is that what we are dealing with here is a masterly Plan, surprising in its perfection. A perfect Plan. *The* perfect Plan. Yes, that's the best way to describe it.'

He went and sat in the armchair at his desk. He was silent a while, smoking.

'And now I must digress,' he said. 'There are a lot of zig-zags here as you may perhaps have noticed, but there's no other way, because we have to see, clearly and completely, the area in which the Plan will work, in which we shall make it work. We must see what are the given facts, and how they justify Central's decision to use the Plan in this particular case. What are the matters we must consider? First of all, the note sent to me this morning by an unknown informer; you know about that. We have no facts to indicate whether the note is valid or a hoax. Thus I took the first step of sending agents to the Café Sport, to see if anything would happen there. I wasn't far wrong in thinking the note valid. The man whose description we had did in fact come to the Café Sport. The unfortunate thing was that we didn't take him alive. Let us call him Suspect No. 1, who is— or was, if you prefer—guilty. Now, as far as Suspect No. 2 is concerned, I can't be sure. One possibility is that his meeting with Suspect No. 1 in the café was by chance. A second possibility is that it wasn't by chance and he

was precisely the one who was to meet with the first—
he was in fact his accomplice. But we don't have any relevant facts. Not just relevant, we don't have any facts at
all about him and that's the truth. We can't delay his
questioning until kingdom come. He'll suspect something sooner or later if we carry on delaying his con-
frontation with the other one; he'll suspect he doesn't
exist. Or that he wasn't caught in the end, or even that
what happened to him was what in fact *did* happen to
him. That would be a catastrophe. We could let him
go. As I say, we have no evidence. We could let him go
and then follow him systematically. And naturally, we
also have the possibility of questioning him further, and
indeed with... all the well-known powers of questioning
at our disposal. But if he's cunning—and that's not out
of the question—then seeing that the other man remains
invisible, he'll guess that something suspicious is going
on, that we have nothing against him, and he'll bear up.
Maybe he won't yield to any form of deep interrogation.
Unless he, too, dies on our hands under questioning.
Then we're still nowhere. These are all possibilities and
problems. At this point, Central stepped in and ordered
me to put the Plan into operation. A Plan that will be
used for the first time, and by us. Yes, I've known about
the Plan for some time. Last February, at Central, at the
special conference of all local chiefs in the capital, they
told us about the Plan and explained exactly what it
was. It's the first time, I tell you again, that the Plan will

be put into operation and will be tested for future use. The honour and the responsibility are as heavy as can be! You understand me, I'm sure. I don't know who is or are the creators of the Plan. It's not out of the question that it's the creation of an electronic brain, as I think I said before. I'm very excited, I have a passion for the Plan that we are about to execute for the first time, and I may say the same things over and over again, it doesn't matter. What matters is that the Plan is a masterpiece, and I say so with all my heart! You will set out by Special Branch car tomorrow morning to bring the man in custody to Central the same day—or, supposedly the same day. That's what I've told our man, that he'll be brought to Central the same day. Now I've left him in peace, and I shall leave him in peace until they drive him into the inner courtyard for the interrogation. And the two of you are completely unknown to our man; you'll meet him for the first time in the morning. You will pretend to be a straightforward agent, one of the many agents of Special Branch, just like the Manager. Be careful! It's important, this: it mustn't seem that you're any different from the Manager, that you're an interrogator. You'll call the Manager "colleague" and the Manager will call you "colleague." And, indeed, on the way to the harbour for the ferry, when the Manager's driving, you'll find an opportunity to tell our man that you've agreed between you to share the driving, that's to say *you'll* be driving to the capital when you leave the ferry. From the time you set out, the two of you will behave towards our man in what is called a "friendly manner." Be careful, though! Don't overdo it! Nothing in particular that might make him suspect it was unnatural, not straightforward. Take it easy, but be on your guard. You owe it to the Plan to carry it out masterfully. Keep your mind on the details! At a first hurried glance, the Plan seems strange, very strange, illogical. But that's exactly where its strength lies! It's like punching your opponent very calmly at exactly the moment he least suspects it. This one unexpected punch will lay him out more certainly than a direct attack. So now, let's see just what the Plan is.'

He went to the radiator and ran his hand along its bars as if stroking it, then turned to me.

'The responsibility falls on you,' he said. 'To begin with, both you and the Manager will be working together on the Plan. You will create, gently as we said, an atmosphere not exactly friendly, but cordial. But later you will be on your own with our man, and all the responsibility will be yours. According to the Plan, we shall exploit this sudden change in temperature towards the prisoner. In particular: this man was arrested suddenly while drinking the brandy he'd ordered in the Café Sport. Is he guilty? Not guilty? We can't say yes or no with certainty. Immediately after his arrest, he finds himself in Special Branch. It's as if he went suddenly from a high temperature to a low. An object that has been suddenly cooled. Now there's a question tormenting him: "What will happen to me at Central?" His transfer to the capital must be—this is foreseen by the Plan—an unexpected rise in temperature for him. The heart-warming sensation that will be created, the very everyday atmosphere as if nothing was happening, that, too, will warm him. Then, when he finally arrives in the capital, he'll fall again into the cold. This is our point! It's as if we have a pipe which we will subject to sudden changes of temperature—hot, cold, hot, cold. Eventually, the pipe will crack. The Plan applies this pipe experiment to the Café Sport man: our man is the pipe. We apply to him a high temperature and then freezing cold. And we expect, with certainty, that our man, the pipe, will crack. So tomorrow, when we arrive at Central—not tomorrow, the day after, I mean—or even earlier maybe, our man will break. With the first interrogation at Central, or even without interrogation, because of the crack that's been made in him, revelations will come out which we couldn't get by any other method. Chiefly because we don't have any facts against him, and the other Café Sport man had that misfortune—a misfortune for the Special Branch, I say again—of dying before the appropriate time.'

'The Plan, I see it now, I feel it taking its full form inside me,' I said. 'Astonishing!'

'I'm very pleased!' said the Chief. 'It's unnecessary to emphasise that if the Plan works, that will mean good luck for all of us. I hope you understand me. The Special

Branch knows how to reward its capable people, those who are passionately devoted to it.'

'All shall happen as it should!' I assured him.

'A basic part of the Plan, perhaps the most basic, is that for anything to happen, nothing must seem to happen.'

I looked at him enquiringly. 'That last point, I must beg you to explain,' I said.

He didn't explain at once. He took a little box of toothpicks out of his desk drawer and started to clean his teeth, without putting up his other hand to cover what he was doing. I didn't find it a very pleasant sight. If it hadn't been the Chief, I would have expressed my displeasure.

'It's very simple,' he continued, with the toothpick between his lips like a cigarette. 'The Plan must proceed gently, as I said before. You, who have to play the main part, must take care to be relaxed, just as if you were gently breathing. As for success, it will come by itself, I'm certain, if you're careful to avoid the number one enemy of the Plan, which is anything remarkable. Everything rolls along as if nothing were happening. That's why I said just now that for the Plan the most fundamental requirement is that nothing happens. Nothing noticeable. If you can manage that point, then success is guaranteed. The Plan isn't a storm, a squall, breaking out in a rage and then passing. No, the Plan is a gentle, steady rain, falling slowly and watering the soil to its depths. And suddenly, just when you don't expect it, comes the collapse! It's just that collapse we want to produce in the Café Sport man. He will collapse internally at a given moment, lose his balance, and talk. Certainly, we're playing a card. A card whose ultimate value we don't know. But in life—and in the Special Branch—we must be daring, take risks. What else can I tell you? I think I've told you everything, at least the basics. The best you can do is use the Plan as a guide, and at the same time use your imagination. The Plan is the base on which you will build. As for the various technical details, for instance, how you will present the so-called faulty distributor to our man and what you will do then, how you'll walk to the town, where you'll stay... We've reserved a room at the Grand National in complete secrecy. It's a hotel we trust. A suitable room for the circumstances, on the top floor, the seventh. Room 717. Anyway, we'll discuss all the details soon. All four of us. Yes, four. Me, you two, and one other, the fourth, an agent I haven't chosen yet and who will come into action when the Manager is supposed to be at the workshop. He will follow you and our man from the Café Sport when you go out for a walk in town. Oh, yes: in the middle there's a walk in the town. For the duration of the walk, you'll have to play your part with the greatest possible perfection. You will have to pretend that you, too, are a person with feelings, to play the role of a *person*. You understand: gently, without exaggeration, as if you're really in the company of a friend and you've gone out for a walk in the town. Don't do anything special or impressive. Above all, he must not suspect that any of this is planned. What will happen in the end I don't know. It's certainly possible that at some moment he'll try to escape. I don't need to tell you what to do in such circumstances. Anyway, you'll have the backing of the other, who will be following you unseen but ready for action in time of need. Be careful not to have the accident we had with his partner in crime. If there's no alternative but to shoot him, aim for the legs so that we can bring him in wounded. In conclusion, whatever happens, the Plan will succeed! Either our man will break under the continual changes of temperature, and especially with your fake friendliness, with the warmth he'll feel during the walk in the town, or he'll break and open his little mouth, sooner or later, at Central. Or if he tries to escape, we're there. If he tries to make a run for it, then we have his confession of guilt from his own hands. And then he will be obliged willy-nilly to make further revelations. All in all, whatever happens, we're in the right position. The Plan is—I say it again and I shall say it repeatedly—a flawless Plan.'

'What would you say to a second sandwich?'

We were right in front of the window of a cake shop when he made the suggestion.

'I'd say yes and gobble it down at once.'

He went to order but I got there first.

'What would you prefer, ham or cheese?'

'Cheese. But next time I'll pay,' he said.

'OK, next time I'll let you treat me.'

At the first corner the light happened to be red. As we were waiting, I looked behind me carefully. I saw the other chap take something from the same cake shop, but I don't think it was a sandwich. Now I felt calm. I knew he was following closely and I wouldn't be alone in case of need.

'I suggest we sit and drink something refreshing,' I said. 'We still have ten minutes left of the full hour we agreed for our walk. What do you say?'

'OK. The sandwich will make us thirsty, so I'll happily offer you a cold juice.'

'Ah, I'm with you now,' I smiled. 'I accept your offer, though I won't take a juice but an iced coffee.'

On the opposite pavement there was a row of cafés with tables outside and multi-coloured umbrellas against the sun. Umbrellas with advertisements for such-and-such make of beer or orangeade or razor blades that lasted for fifteen shaves and so on.

We went and took a table at the Progress Café, right on the edge of the pavement.

That juice at the Progress Café was far too cold. And now that he'd just drunk it—he'd emptied half the glass in one go—he felt something in his throat. *A fine time for my tonsils to get inflamed!* he said to himself. Then he reflected that it was ridiculous, idiotic, to sit and worry about his tonsils just when he was being led straight into the lion's den. At full speed, too! Tomorrow morning he'd be in the capital. How would he find his way through with those vultures lying in wait for him at Central!

He sank back into the oddly comfortable canvas chair. He saw the agent calmly drinking his iced coffee with a straw. A moment later he made a movement with his hand to chase away the fly that, leaving the agent's nose, landed on his own. He half closed his right eye. Since childhood, whenever he wanted to think hard, to concentrate, to put his thoughts in order, he did the same. It was automatic—a tic—he half closed his right eye.

After their love-making on the tiled floor, he went to the mirror and started to dress. In the opposite corner, all bedraggled after their struggle, he watched her fastening her bra.

'Why are you gazing at yourself in the mirror?' she asked.

'That scar below my ear... it's bleeding. Not much; it always bleeds. I suspect some little teeth. Very sharp, fierce little teeth.'

She didn't say anything, just gave a gurgling laugh and went to the other side of the bed and lit the lamp. His room was on the ground floor, and the window— the only one—looked onto the road. They'd had to close the window and the shutters. If not, any passer-by would have feasted his eyes and ears.

She took up her stocking—one of them, the right, was already on—and examined it in the light. 'Catastrophe!' she said. 'It's got a run, at least ten centimetres. And tell me, my sweet, why did you bite my breast? That gives me the right to bite you wherever I like. You can thank me that I bit you on the scar and not somewhere else. Now we're even!'

Then they talked about when they'd meet again. Her idea was for a second meeting the same day. He was enthusiastic, so that evening there would be a repeat performance of their entertaining game, whose premiere matinée had occurred between three and five.

'And where will you go now?' he asked her.

'The dressmaker. I've got a fitting for my autumn suit. First of the season! You know, the green and brown we chose together last week. And where will *you* go?'

'Where will I go? Nowhere special. Until Monday, when I go back to work, the office doesn't exist and I'm free. I think I'll just wander about. Gaze in the shop windows, at the posters outside the cinema... I don't know yet where I'll go. All I know is I need some fresh air. To move around, to recover from the storm that has torn me to bits.'

They looked knowingly at each other.

'What time shall we meet? I need an hour and a half at the dressmakers at least. Six thirty, quarter to seven at the latest, I reckon to finish. Let's say seven o'clock on the dot.'

'Agreed. At the post office?'

'Why not?'

'OK, seven o'clock in the hall of the post office, in front of Foreign Registered for a change; not always at Parcels.'

She left first. Then he went to the window and half-pulled the curtain—he saw it had holes in two or three places and needed mending. Through the grilles of the shutters he watched her go across the road, crossing Chrysanthemum Street diagonally, finally turning right at the second corner. Not the second; the third.

In a little while he left, too, and went straight to the Café Sport. Until seven, when they'd meet at the post office, he had something particular to do. Very particular and very secret.

Very easy, if he wanted to sit at any of the tables immediately inside the entrance. But the message had been clear: to choose a table deep inside, against the big mirror, and with his right leg stretched out. That way anybody not taking care and happening to pass would be sure to tread on it.

All clear! Tables free at the end of the room and against the mirror. Most people frequented cafés after eight.

He sat and waited, according to his instructions: sit and wait. Oh yes, there was something else in the instructions: he should order a double brandy and use the paper from his cigarette packet to draw something. Anything he liked. As for the other, he would make his appearance between 6.15 and 6.30.

No, he didn't know him. And he himself was unknown to the man, but they had enough information to recognise each other: the table far down in the room and against the mirror, the right foot stretched out, the double brandy, the drawing on the paper from the cigarette packet and—above all—the dialogue. The prearranged dialogue that they'd have between them when the other, in passing and as if by chance, would tread on his foot.

He had learnt the dialogue by heart. If the other gave the correct answers, word for word, then yes, he would be the one he was waiting for.

Then he'd let him leave the Café Sport. He knew the other would turn left onto Independence Avenue towards the crossing with National Library Street. At the crossing, by the lights, the man would stand and wait for him. Meanwhile, he'd pay for his double brandy, leave the café in turn and proceed at his own pace to the same place. He'd get there in time to stand next to him. They'd cross the road together, as if they were unconnected. As they walked, the other would whisper to him the time and place for tomorrow's meeting of members. It was one of the most important meetings, and the organisation had been planning it in dark secrecy. Then they would separate discretely. After he'd go quickly to the post office. Seven o'clock they'd said, at the window for Foreign Registered.

Around 6.20 he started to consider the possibility that the meeting would go wrong. The other might not come. For some reason that he couldn't know, maybe there was danger. If he didn't appear by 6.30 at the latest, at 6.31 he would be free to get up and go. The organisation had a way of letting him know what to do next. But for now, there was no reason to think of failure. The other had ten whole minutes yet.

When he suddenly felt someone tread on his right foot, he was sure the man he was waiting for had come. But the test must go according to plan; the crucial thing was the dialogue.

'You trod on me, sir!' he pretended to complain.

The other looked at him as if he didn't know what to think. 'I did?' he said.

OK so far! That 'I did?' was the first thing the contact had to say.

'Yes, you! And you trod on my right foot which has—'

'Excuse me!' he interrupted. 'You see, I'm short-sighted; and I'm afraid that, lately...'

He didn't even take any notice of what else he said: *this* other was not *the* other he was waiting for.

It was 6.25 and still nothing! Would he come straight in from outside or was he already in the Café Sport? Perhaps he was already here, already at a table and waiting for the right moment, the moment he would choose himself.

He took a look round the room, pretending he wasn't doing it with any purpose, just absent-mindedly. Could he be one of those three young men talking about the film *The Beauty of the Night*? Why not? He might not be alone in the Café Sport; he might have company. Or maybe he was one of the customers on his own? That was most likely. Those two salesmen who'd started an endless conversation about the price of cooking fat, with continual gestures and calculations and crossings-out on a greasy pad? And if he was one of those two and all that talk about the price of cooking fat was camouflage? Or it might be one of those two old men who were secretly looking at photographs—was it just a show?

Then, 6.29 by the Café Sport clock, and 6.31 by his watch. He wasn't sure which of the two was right, but by now the chances of his not turning up were greater. Maybe something unforeseen had happened to stop him. He thought also that it wasn't out of the question that he was in the café but had noticed suspicious movements; Special Branch agents might also be stationed in the café and so he couldn't make his appearance.

At that moment he saw someone come out of the toilet—felt rather than saw—and leave the door half open. Irritated as he was with this pointless waiting, he would have made some remark about the door, but he decided against it. The one who'd come out of the toilet came forward between the tables, passing right beside his, and stood on his right foot. Heavily, too, so that he cried out.

'You trod on me, sir!' he said. His mind was racing.

'I did?' he said, a tall man, about forty years old, with glasses and an unremarkable face.

'Yes, and you trod on my right foot, which has a corn.'

'Really?' he said sarcastically. 'Believe me, I thought it was the left,' and he continued towards the exit.

He left him a little time, got out some change for the brandy and glanced over at the waiter. According to his instructions, he should leave two minutes later, meet him on the corner of Independence Avenue and National Library Street... then suddenly he saw virtually on top of him one of the two cooking-fat salesmen who took out a yellow identity card from his pocket and gave him to understand who he was dealing with.

As the agent on his right was going towards the exit of the Café Sport, he remembered the drawing. Everything had happened so unexpectedly that he'd forgotten it. But now he wanted it, wanted to have those two little circles with him—her breasts. Not to abandon them unkindly on the cold marble, to be dirtied by the waiter's rag as he wiped up the water and the cigarette butts. He thought of asking the agent if he could go back and get the drawing, but changed his mind at once. No, he shouldn't take the risk—put her at risk. The agent would look at the drawing and suspect that those two little circles were somehow subversive, against the Regime, and they'd become evidence against him and he'd have another problem. If he told them they were her breasts, they'd ask to see them, to investigate them, to touch them and measure them, to see if her breasts were as in the drawing, a touch uneven, the left bigger than the right.

At the revolving door of the Café Sport the agent whispered to him, 'We'll both go in the same compartment. It'll be a squash, but never mind.'

And so it was. Stuck together in the little space, and the agent smelt bad. Not of cooking fat but sweat.

'We have a car for our own use,' he informed him as they went out, 'but it's parked two blocks further on.'

They went down Independence Avenue, the agent always on his right. And he didn't notice at first that another agent was walking to his left so that they had him in between them. The other agent had silently appeared from somewhere, as if he was by chance at his side.

When they reached the first corner it looked to him as if people were running towards the other side of the avenue, near the Astron Cinema.

After the first shock at the intervention of the Special Branch, all his energy went into staying alert. He must sacrifice everything to stay calm, be in control of himself, order his nerves to obey him. Because first of all, he didn't know the meaning of his arrest. A tip-off? Maybe. The strongest possibility was that they'd been shopped. What had become of the other man? Had he got away? Or had they arrested him too outside the Café Sport? He'd seen him going past the tables and into the revolving door... they'd probably trapped him when he came out onto the pavement. But if he'd slipped away from them?

The questions raced around in his head. Was it really a tip-off? Did Special Branch know everything? Had they been stationed in the Café Sport from early on? Or was it something else? What else? As he walked towards the car between the two agents, he agonised over what might have happened. How could he get a clue? He even considered the possibility that his arrest was entirely unconnected with the meeting in the Café Sport and the organisation. Maybe there was something else that he didn't know about and he'd find out when they got him to Special Branch. The conclusion of all his thoughts and considerations was, again, that above all he must keep calm. He was in danger of betraying himself if he lost control. Such things happened often. Someone was arrested, in fact guilty of crime A, but the arrest was not for that, he was arrested by chance or for crime B, and he'd lose control, rush, or seem arrogant, and he himself would reveal that he was guilty of crime A, while the interrogator had no idea, not even a suspicion, that he had in his hands the culprit they'd been searching for in vain for so long.

'Here we are!' said the agent, the one who'd arrested him, in front of a car with four seats and two doors.

He got into the rear seat, as they gestured for him to do, with the other agent.

The car showed no sign of being anything out of the ordinary. Normal number-plates, everything normal.

As they crossed Independence Avenue on their way— he knew of course where Special Branch offices were, a modern building in Theatre Square which gave the impression of being some company's offices or something of that sort—they had to pass the post office. He felt troubled as they passed. He reflected that if this unforeseen event hadn't happened, he'd be in the post office now, not passing by in a car. He'd be in the hall, in front of Foreign Registered.

He looked through the window, which was firmly closed despite the heat. If only he could see her, just for a second! Ah, no! Better that she shouldn't happen to pass just now. If she suddenly saw him in an unknown car, with two unknown people, if she caught sight of him, expressionless and unspeaking, not even gesturing to her with hands or eyes, she'd be crazy with worry. She wouldn't know what to suppose, what to think.

He looked at his watch discreetly: 7.02.

'Does the gentleman have a rendezvous?' asked the agent in the seat to his right sarcastically.

'No! A rendezvous? What rendezvous? I just looked at my watch automatically.'

He felt ashamed of himself for the haste with which he'd denied having a rendezvous. It was as if he'd betrayed her. But what could he say? At all costs he must conceal her, keep her in the shadows. Not mix her up in his adventures. She had no idea about all that. He'd told her that from the time they separated until seven when they'd meet again, he'd go for a walk with no particular aim, no programme. He hadn't told her the truth. How could he tell her the truth?

When they reached Special Branch offices they turned into a small entrance—small in comparison with the main entrance. There were four or five other cars there, in an inner courtyard.

'Journey's end!' said the agent who had arrested him, trying a touch of humour.

Whatever was hidden behind his arrest, it must be an adventure whose outcome he couldn't foresee. Special Branch, whose only purpose was the defence of the Regime, was the highest authority in the land, and its powers limitless. It was not bound in any way by considerations of justice and so on. If you had the misfortune to fall into its hands for whatever reason, it was impossible to escape.

Keep calm! he ordered himself once more as they passed through the entrance.

The two agents led him to the lift.

'I hope you're taking me straight to the superior officer,' he said to the cooking-fat salesman.

No answer.

They got out at the third floor and went to the end of the corridor, to the last door but one on the right. The agent—not the salesman—opened the door; it wasn't locked, and they went together into the room, which was like a doctor's waiting room or some such.

The agent told him to sit down. 'It's not obligatory,' he hastened to add. 'If you want to...'

'I prefer to stand. I won't sit down. I want to see the superior officer straight away. I don't know what's going on, why you're giving me this trouble.'

The agent looked at him silently, then opened a magazine, one of the many on a low table in the corner by the radiator, and flipped through the pages. As for the other one, the salesman, he'd left them as soon as they'd reached the door. He shortly reappeared, carrying a change of clothes—suit, underwear—and a pair of shoes.

'You must undress,' he told him. 'Completely.'

He thought of complaining, but what for?

The two agents watched him as he undressed.

'Underwear, too?' he asked.

'Underwear, too. And your watch.'

He put on the underwear they gave him, and the suit. The trousers especially were very wide and he thought himself a very funny figure with the suit flapping round him. As for the shoes, they were rather better; his size at least.

The agents took his own clothes and shoes.

'You'll be left alone, but not for long,' said the salesman. 'We'll be back soon to take you to the Chief. I might as well inform you that the window doesn't open, so I advise you not to try anything... nor the door either. No, the door won't be locked, but quite simply you won't open it. If you need anything, there's a bell over the electricity socket, on the right in the corner, and you can ring.'

They turned to leave. The salesman stopped in the doorway, 'If you need to go to the toilet,' he said, 'say so now.'

He said no, not urgently. Then the door closed. He heard their footsteps fading away down the corridor.

For a little while he stayed standing up. He went over to the window. Closed, and the shutters, too. He wondered if he really couldn't open it. There was no sign that it had been secured in such a way as to not open. But they might, he thought, have connected it to the electricity. High voltage, so that if you touched the handle you'd get a big shock.

There wasn't the slightest sound from the neighbouring rooms. Was there no-one in the other offices? Or had they some sort of soundproofing? Only from the corridor he heard footsteps now and then.

He looked at the pictures on the wall. Four in all. Tourist photographs, snowy scenes, sunshiny places, etc. He went up and looked at them one by one.

Maybe one of these innocent pictures—or more than one—had a hole, very small, but big enough to watch him from the next room. To spy on his smallest movement, the slightest change in his expression or eye-movement. He couldn't know, he couldn't be sure of anything in here.

He sat on the chair near the window. He must show complete calm, not even a nervous twitch of his fingers. To wait peacefully, as if he had no uneasiness, like a person with a clear conscience and no fear. Soon, when they took him to the superior officer, the matter would be cleared up. Had they arrested him because he was mixed up in the organisation against the Regime, or was it something entirely unrelated? Most likely they'd arrested him because of his meeting with the other man. They'd been shopped, who knows by whom or when. Or why.

The door opened. Strange, he hadn't heard any footsteps in the corridor.

'The Chief is waiting for you in his office,' the agent told him; another agent unknown to him.

No, there was nothing to reproach himself for during all the Chief's interrogation—he'd looked like a nobody by his manner and his glasses—and he'd kept completely calm from the very beginning.

'I'm waiting for your view of events,' were the first words the Chief had said to him. 'The other man, your accomplice, gave us his view just now. Some very interesting facts emerged from this preliminary investigation, but I want to make a comparison with the view you have yourself.'

'My accomplice!' he said very firmly and looking straight at the Chief. 'I don't understand what you're saying.'

'I should, I think, put matters plainly from the start,' continued the Chief. 'It seems that I haven't made myself clear, probably my fault. The point is you had an encounter in the Café Sport. It was preceded by a small accident, when a clumsy person stood on your right foot.'

'Ah, you're talking about that absent-minded man. He explained that he's short-sighted—'

'No!' he interrupted. 'I don't mean the first person who stood on your foot; I'm interested in the second one.'

Something ran down his spine like mercury. Like lightning he realised he'd made a gaffe; it would have been better not to talk about the first one, wanting to shield the other; he should rather have asked the Chief at once, 'Which of the two do you mean? You see it was just my evening at the Café Sport: two people trod on my foot!'

'I hope now I've made myself clear,' continued the Chief, and polished his glasses on the curtain.

'Yes. I mean, I understand that the second chap has some special significance for you which I'm naturally not in a position to know.'

'Not "naturally"! But let us assume for the moment that that's how it is, that you're not in a position, etc. But you must certainly know what you said to him and what he said to you.'

In a few seconds he considered what would be best: to make something up or to repeat the conversation word for word. If the Special Branch already had the full dialogue in its possession, he would be in a difficult position. If it wasn't like that, but that the agents—the salesmen—had only heard the dialogue word by word and the Chief was setting a trap for him, to see if he changed anything, then...

'I have no objection to telling you exactly what we said. Well, when the man came out of the toilet—my table was right next to the toilet and I was annoyed because eight or nine out of ten people coming out left the door open or half open... what was I saying? Ah yes, this man who was unknown to me came out of the toilet leaving the door half open. I considered saying something to him about it, but I said nothing so as not to start a conversation and get more annoyed. Then, as he was passing, he stood on my right foot, just like the man before. Just at that moment I was bending down to look for change for my brandy.'

'And what was your dialogue?'

'It's not hard to remember! I said to him in an irritated manner, "You trod on me, sir." "I did?" he said, as if he hadn't understood. "Yes, and you trod on my right foot, which has a corn!" He smiled ironically and said "Really? Believe me, I thought it was the left." And he turned and went away.'

The Chief remained silent a little, then he went and opened a file on his desk and read something.

'Very good!' he said. 'The dialogue was exactly as you told us. Our agents have it written down here word for word. There's not one difference. There is however a question: Why did you let him go without saying anything further, to give him the answer he deserved, since he'd made a joke of it?'

'Why should I start a conversation with him? I thought of it for a moment, then changed my mind. I don't like arguments, you understand...'

'And you insist that this man is unknown to you?'
'Yes.'
'Where would you have gone after leaving the café?'
'Home,' he said shortly. 'To my room.'

'I see. The point is that you insist on your complete ignorance. The man who stood on your foot, the second one, is unknown to you and you don't have any business with him. That's what you're saying, agreed?'

'Yes.'

'What would you say if you learnt that the man we're talking about is in an organisation against the Regime and we were following him? You were the only person to have contact with him in the Café Sport.'

'I have nothing to add. His activities against the Regime don't concern me. I repeat: I'm not guilty.'

'That's where we disagree!' said the Chief. '"I'm not guilty" doesn't at all mean "I'm innocent." You understand?'

'No.'

The Chief clapped his hands as if applauding.

'It's very simple,' he continued. '"I'm not guilty" is a negative expression: that is, you insist you have not done something in particular. Here, however, in the case of the Regime, the question is not whether you are or are not guilty, but whether you are or are not innocent. I want to make that clear. He who is innocent is he who can show that he has done something positive for the Regime. Certainly you may not be guilty, you may not be the culprit in offence A or B, and yet be, at the same time, not innocent.'

'I am a peace-loving citizen', he said as if reading from a text.

'I'm sorry to see that the misunderstanding continues. I don't argue about your being a peace-loving citizen. The investigation which our agents have been conducting from the moment they brought you here has come to the same conclusion: you are a peace-loving citizen. But that is not enough for us to be able to say that you are innocent. It's just here that the matter becomes complicated, and I ask you, what is the particular thing you have done in support of the Regime?'

'An example would help me to consider that. I mean, what might I have done but have failed to do?'

The Chief went and sat at his desk and buried his head in his hands.

'You have nothing to bring forward to show that you have done something positive for the Regime. That's the point.'

'I never gave the smallest ground for complaint. As I say: I am a peace-loving citizen.'

'Enough!' shouted the Chief, banging his fist on the glass-topped desk. 'And *I* say: that's *not* enough! It's not enough to be "a peace-loving citizen". "Peace-loving citizens" are not supporters of the Regime, but those who make efforts on behalf of the Regime are. All right, I'll give you the example you want: how many people, up to now, have you denounced to Special Branch for activity, or simply ideology or feelings, not in alignment with the Regime?'

He made no reply to the question.

'There's no need to hurry! I understand, you want to work out exactly how many you've denounced and naturally that takes a little time.'

'No.'

'But?'

'I haven't denounced anybody. I'm sorry, but the truth is that I've not denounced anybody, ever.'

Now it was the Chief who remained silent.

'Why, please?' he asked after two minutes in a very kindly way, as if afraid of upsetting him.

'The occasion has never arisen. Me, I'm a—'

'—"peace-loving citizen", the Chief completed for him. 'We recognise that, but it doesn't prove anything! And fundamentally, it doesn't prove that you're inno- cent. For the Special Branch, people are divided into two mutually exclusive categories: those who are with the Regime and those who are not with the Regime. It's not necessary for anyone to be a declared enemy of the Regime, it's merely enough that he isn't *with* the Regime, and then, automatically, naturally, he is its en- emy. The philosophy of the Special Branch is simple and uncompromising: "He who is not with me is against me".'

He saw the Chief's eyes staring at him.

'"He who is not with me is against me"' said the Chief again. 'You know the saying? You know who said it?'

'Yes: Hitler.'

The Chief laughed out loud.

'No, Hitler didn't say it. Christ said it. Don't look at me so wide-eyed! Christ said it.'

'I had no idea. And after all, I have no idea what you're accusing me of.'

'And what about this here?'

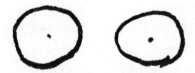

He felt a trembling when he saw the two little circles. He thought the sketch had stayed on the table in the Café Sport. Some other agent, maybe the second sales-man, must have taken the sketch after his arrest, he rea-soned. He made an effort to smile.

'It's two small circles,' he said.

'Thank you very much! I can see it's two small circles. But what meaning do these two small circles have?'

'No meaning at all. Just two small circles, nothing more. To pass the time, I took the paper from my cigarette packet and... Ah, no, don't tell me you find those two small circles suspicious! I could have drawn two small squares or two small triangles.'

The Chief looked at the sketch and seemed not to be satisfied.

'And who can guarantee for me that it's not a suspicious diagram? That it's not two hidden, two secret arms stores which will be used at some given time against the Regime?'

'It's two small circles.'

'Take off your right shoe. And sock.'

He looked at the Chief as if he hadn't heard and wanted it repeated.

'I said, take off your right shoe and sock. And the left shoe and sock.'

He did as the Chief asked, who then approached him and examined his feet, first the right, then the other.

'Yes, you really do have a corn on the right foot,' he told him, 'and you don't have one on the left. Thus, I have nothing more to say about that.'

He passed a sleepless night. How could he close his eyes after the news the Chief had given him when they had taken him back to his office just after ten? 'Tomorrow morning they'll take you to the capital. Orders from Central. Your accomplice is already on the way, accompanied of course, to Central. The facts that emerged from his interrogation are such that his immediate transfer to Central was thought necessary. I have nothing further to do with Operation Café Sport. Central has taken the matter in hand.'

No, he didn't expect to hear that! From the moment he heard that he was to be transferred to Central, he was on his guard. Some instinct flared up in him: don't let them take him to Central! That would be a dead end, a definite dead end. Certainly, this transfer didn't bode well. What might have happened? Why didn't they interrogate him here, confront him with the other man? He tried to keep track of things in the darkness in which he found himself; he considered all the given possibilities. Maybe the other had confessed and his revelations were, or were supposed to be, so important that Central wanted him urgently? It wasn't out of the question. The Special Branch was not in the habit of conducting its interrogations with kid gloves, no indeed! Nor did he feel too comforted with the way they had interrogated him up to now. On the contrary, their politeness seemed to him suspect, as if they were preparing to deliver a knock-out blow. But maybe they hadn't used the same methods in interrogating the other man. Maybe they'd subjected him to an exhausting interrogation, and finally he'd broken down. Or maybe they hadn't subjected him to anything, they'd simply found something incriminating in his pockets? Incriminating for both of them? How could he know! What if the other man had documents or memoranda on him, clearly showing his, or their, guilt? Or some chance matter had betrayed him, some detail which he couldn't get out of? Or if the other man was—and this idea obsessed and tortured him—yes, suppose that man were playing a double game, if he in fact worked for Special Branch and had got mixed up in the organisation on their orders? He tried to dismiss the idea, but it was impossible. It had fixed it-self as if by hooks into his mind and was a terrible night-mare. If he were a Special Branch man, an agent...

He thought of opening the window to see how far along the night was. He might be able to guess the time. 'It's as well to bear in mind that the window's locked...' They'd given him that information, or warning, when they had taken him in the room. No, he mustn't give them any reason to suspect him. And at the first chance, he'd make a move—*the* move. On the journey to the capital they'd be bound to give him an opportunity to escape.

When he'd heard the Chief say that they were going to move him in the morning, he nearly gave himself away. But he pretended to be indifferent. Not indifferent, but annoyed that now there'd be a prolonging of this ordeal. And as if he hadn't heard his complaint, the Chief leant down to talk into the intercom. He informed the two agents that they would accompany him. First, the one he called the Manager, and then another with whom they discussed some 'Operation Toilet Paper'. In the end, the Chief had him brought to his office to dis-cuss 'Operation Café Sport'.

He would put on an act; during the journey he'd pre-tend to be a peaceful little lamb until the moment he'd make his escape. The least he could expect at Central was death. But how, and when, would he reach that death? He'd first have to go through a series of interrogations, a tangle of interrogations with the special method he'd heard that they used at Central.

The truth was he didn't pass the night entirely sleeplessly; sleep overcame him for a bit. He was in the armchair and a kind and gentle sleep like a child's crept up on him. He realised it when he woke up; a door slammed somewhere and it shattered both his sleep and his dream. Because he *had* had a dream: he dreamt he had fallen asleep and was dreaming. The door slamming like a pistol shot dissolved it; it turned the dream to dust and left not the slightest trace of the dream within a dream.

'The time's ten past three. That means our walk is over. And anyway, we've even had five minutes extra. I took the initiative in telling you our time's up, because I want to be correct. Don't want you to suppose I'm abusing the rules...'

The agent laughed, and took the straw from the coffee he'd drunk and fiddled with it.

'Don't worry!' he told him. 'Who's to check up on you? I'm the only one responsible; I bear the whole responsibility for our walk, it was my idea. So it's me you'd have to deal with.

'I can't work out how it got to ten past three—twelve past.'

'Waiter, what do we owe?'

'Waiter, what do we owe?' he said, repeating the agent's gesture and question.

The waiter stood between them and didn't know who to deal with.

'Won't you let me pay?'

'Ah, no; I hope you're keeping our agreement. Didn't we say the other time that I would treat you?'

'Well, since you insist...'

While the Café Sport man was checking the bill, the agent took the opportunity to furtively adjust his pistol, which had gone sideways. He didn't want his companion to see what he was doing. According to the Plan, he must positively avoid any reminder that he was a prisoner, and that he had opposite or right beside him his guard, armed and ready. Ready, should the need arise, to shoot him with a small and uncompromising bullet.

'I've settled the bill and we can leave.'

They went as far as the corner, where the agent stopped.

'I have something to suggest,' he said, 'that is, to extend our walk. Let's say a one-hour extension. What do you say?'

'I have no objection; it's up to you. If you like, then yes, and if not, we can go straight back to the Grand National.'

'Well, let's not hang about any longer. Our walk has an hour's extension.'

'Agreed.'

'And where do you think we should go? Any special suggestions?'

'No.'

'I think the best is to do what we've been doing up to now, that's to say, no programme: just go where our feet lead us.'

They went up University Avenue. At the crossing with Victory Avenue they turned right and took the left-hand pavement which was out of the sun.

They talked about various things, jumping from one subject to another.

'I've something to suggest to you,' said the Interrogator. 'I'm full of suggestions today.'

'I'm listening.'

'That we talk to each other in the singular. I don't know, this formality of the plural form annoys me.

'Certainly! I accept your suggestion gratefully.'[1]

---

[1] The Greek custom is to reflect social distinction linguistically through the use of the singular "you" for informal situations with the plural "you" reserved for strangers, elders, and figures of authority.

One girl had rust-coloured hair. The other, too, had rust-coloured hair. There was, however, one small difference: the second, when I made an impromptu interrogation, broke down and confessed that hers wasn't its natural colour. She firmly refused to reveal what colour it had been to begin with, but admitted that she'd dyed it so that it would be the same colour as her friend's, which was its natural colour, etc., etc. Note that all this happened much later, an hour and a half after we'd met them, when all four of us were lying down on our backs, or our stomachs, on the burning sand. There was a lot of good sand, but there was rubbish too—empty tins and greaseproof paper with remnants of food and various other things.

Taking things in order, what happened first was that we met them. There was nothing special about the meeting, it happened very simply and naturally, just as two young men, wandering about a fairly large town, get to know two young women wandering the same streets.

I can't say much about our meeting or how from two people we became four. Not because I don't want to say much but because there's not much to say. The only thing I can say is that the two of us had stopped in front of a window—the hundredth or thousandth we'd stopped at—and were looking at the things inside. Smokers' requisites: lighters, cigarette holders, pipes, pipe-cleaners, etc.

He was to my right. My eye was on a gas lighter in very modern style; I liked it a lot and thought of going in to get it.

'How does that lighter in the right-hand corner look to you?' I asked him without turning my head in his direction. 'Do you like it?'

'Certainly, I like it a lot.'

The answer came from a woman's voice. One of the two friends—the one with the dyed hair—had leant down by chance between me and him and so the question seemed to be addressed to her.

'But if you want me to buy it for you, I certainly shan't!' the girl added before I could say a word.

Everything else happened by itself. We teased each other and joked, nothing special, then we asked them— well, *I* asked them—if they had any objection to our keeping them company a while. Their eyes met at once in agreement—strange how women can make silent agreements like that!—and then one of them, the one with naturally rust-coloured hair, answered me.

'To begin with, no, we have no objection. It's just that we planned to go to the beach. This September weather is so unusual that one really must go swimming as long as the summer lasts.'

'What do you say?' I asked him. 'I think the four of us would make good company, even if we two don't go swimming.'

And the two girls together said that it didn't matter that we didn't have swimming costumes, we could rent them at the beach. I explained that we didn't feel like swimming, and in the end we all set out for the beach together.

This unforeseen and refreshing appearance—two young, charming and very lively women—I found very pleasing. I wondered if I should have gone as far as I had. But why not? This new development actually furthered the Plan very well. In a few seconds I considered everything, there in front of the window. Even that the two girls had been set up, to help our man escape at some given moment. Was my worry over the top? No indeed! It might not have been mere chance, our meeting with these two girls. The organisation might have made its own Plan to help our man escape, in which these two charming girls played an important part. I mean, something like what I was doing myself. Finally, however, I had to give up the idea of a trap. The Plan, my Plan, had been kept one hundred percent secret. There was no room for doubt! Therefore, it was impossible that our meeting with the two girls could have some other meaning. So, I must not only dismiss my fears and suspicions but make use of this opportunity which had presented itself so suddenly and at just the right time. An opportunity to create a new warmth in our walk which the two of us had been making in the silent and invisible presence of the third, whom I hadn't seen again since the two of us had left the Progress Café and continued on our walk. I was certain that he was always somewhere near, hidden in the crowd, ready for action should it be necessary. So, even if the two girls were a cunning trick, I still wouldn't be alone; the third one would make his appearance at the critical moment.

But a taxi wouldn't do! The beach was quite a long way away; on foot it would take three quarters of an hour, so that was out of the question. Normally, we'd be able to hail a taxi, but then there'd be the danger that the third man would lose us.

'Now that we've decided to go to the beach together,' he said, 'let's not waste time; let's get the bus.'

Now, on the way to the bus, we were walking in two pairs. He was in front with one girl, and me behind with the other. I had no idea where the bus stop for the beach was, but the two girls told us. From the shop window to the bus stop took about ten minutes.

At one moment, just as we were turning the second corner, I caught sight of the third man coming along behind us. He gave me a smile when our eyes met. Certainly the two girls were a very original development of the Plan, but very useful to it.

There was nothing exceptional about our walk to the bus stop. We didn't stop to look in any shop windows or gaze at interesting things; the girls had told us we needed to hurry as the sun would set at ten past six and they wanted to have a swim before it got dark.

I could hear the conversation of the other two just as well as the conversation I had with my girl—the one with the dyed hair. I considered what an extraordinary piece of luck this meeting with the two girls was. We should have thought of it ourselves at Special Branch and arranged our own girls. Nothing warms things up more than the presence of a woman. But we hadn't thought of it and chance had made up for that.

If the Chief had been somewhere nearby and seen this development of the Plan, he would certainly have been enthusiastic.

In conversation with my girl, as soon as we'd set out from the shop window, I made haste to tell her that my friend and I—a nice touch, that 'my friend'—were just passing through the town on business, and I was quick to add, so as to avoid complications should the other say something different, that our speciality was dealing in cars. I said it all loudly, not as if I were deliberately speaking loudly, just so that the other would hear.

We'd gone some way to the bus stop when, in the midst of conversation with my girl, an idea came back to me: suppose the two girls weren't a chance meeting but agents of the organisation, planning to help the Café Sport man to get away? The idea really tortured me then, but finally I got rid of it for the second time. It just wasn't possible—a chance of one in a thousand million—that they'd found out about the Plan and had arranged the meeting with the girls. I didn't just reject the possibility but I wiped it from my mind completely, along with other worries, and began to enjoy the pleasure that the company of a young and charming woman always brings.

Just before we reached the bus stop, my girl caught her high heel in a drainage grille and it all but snapped off. She gave a little cry, and all four of us stopped. I bent down to see what had happened, and as I was trying to see to the heel—it was nothing serious—I had to hold her foot, first at the ankle and then a little above, and had the pleasure of holding that flesh, sunburnt, firm as a freshly-baked loaf.

While the four of us were going for the bus, the other agent was following at a distance—not so distant that he'd be unable to operate properly in case of need, nor so closely that he'd be noticed and there'd be a danger of ruining the Plan. I must confess, his skill made a big impression on me; his ingenuity in staying unseen but always present in our wanderings about the town with its many and various turnings. When I thought he'd lost us, I'd catch sight of him again in the crowd, or round some corner, or in front of a shop window.

There was a long queue at the bus stop. The four of us stood there, two by two, each with his girl. I didn't see the third man standing in the queue, but I wasn't uneasy; I was sure he was following us like a shadow.

When we got on the bus—we'd had to wait at least a quarter of an hour—I gestured discreetly to the Café Sport man to sit with his girl in a double seat on the right of the gangway, and we two sat immediately behind, so I had him under immediate and complete control.

Nothing remarkable happened on the bus journey. First we went through the working-class areas, then we came out on the big ring-road which would take us straight to the sea.

Although I had passed through the town three times before and knew it quite well, I didn't know the area by the sea. It happened that on the three previous occasions it had been winter or autumn, but late autumn and not like this strange summer-like September.

I don't know why, but as we were going along in the bus I began to have doubts again about this sudden and unplanned extension of the Plan, with two unknown girls met by chance—by chance?—on the street. Maybe my initiative had been a mistake? Again, dark thoughts surrounded me. What if the two girls hadn't been a chance meeting? Had this meeting in front of the tobacconist's been arranged? Had the scenario been set up by the organisation in which the Café Sport man was a member, for the sole purpose of aiding his escape? I couldn't find a proper answer to the questions that sprang up.

No way did they want to jump in the sea unless we went in too.

'That just won't do!' my own girl was the most insistent. 'The four of us came together to the beach, we'll get in the sea together.'

They were so insistent that I confess I started to get annoyed.

'Look, you can hire swimming-trunks by the hour!' explained the other girl, as if we hadn't known.

'I already know that!' I told her.

'Well then, hire them and join us in the sea like decent gentlemen!'

'No!' I said more firmly than before.

'Oh, I see,' she said, 'You're afraid you'll catch something! There's no need to worry, they're pasteurised!'

'Sterilised!' her friend corrected her.

That's how she gave me the idea to put an end to this insistence that was getting on my nerves.

'You guessed it,' I told her. 'You know, I'll tell you something: not me, but my friend, some time ago, the year before last, at a swimming pool in our town— you see there's no sea there and we go swimming in swimming pools—he rented a costume and it took him three months to get over the infection he caught. Since then, the two of us have sworn never to take the chance.'

'Yes, that's the secret,' said the Café Sport man. 'I had a lot of bother. Injections—painful ones. It still hurts, especially when I remember it.'

'Well, since that happened, we won't insist,' said one of them, I don't remember if it was mine or his.

Peace at last! As for the girls, they ran off hand in hand to a cabin to get changed.

We practically had sunstroke—it was hellishly hot!— we waited on the sand for the two girls to come out of the water. Not a chance! One big dive after another, one game after another... time passed, and there we were, stuck on the sand.

'What's this,' I said, 'but a big frustration, to be in the company of two tasty girls beside the sea—practically a summer sea—and not to be able to go swimming.'

'It's up to you to decide, yes or no. I don't have a say.'

'No, I think it's better to stay as we are,' I continued, 'Don't fret! It's nice here. The sea, the boats, the speed-boats, the ships further out, the sardine tins and food wrappers round us and the little children whining and peeing in public...'

'A slice of life! Even if it annoys us, it's certainly a genuine slice of life, warm, spontaneous, unarranged.'

That 'unarranged' set me thinking. Why did he say it? What did it mean, if anything?

In the end, we did get into the sea. We could see that the two girls weren't coming out of the water, in fact they'd gone further out and one moment we could see them, the next not. At some moment, I can't remember who made the first move, me or the Café Sport man, or both of us at once, we got up from our very uncomfortable place, took off our shoes and socks and got into the water ourselves.

We must have made a funny picture because I noticed smiles and whispers around us, but what did we care! We were doing what we wanted and didn't take any account of others! That's what we wanted, to get in the sea wearing our jackets and ties and splash around. Oh, yes, we'd rolled our trousers more or less up to our knees, that's all. It's just that he was wearing long underwear—with green stripes—and I can't say how the sight amused me. He had a lot of trouble with that underwear, trying to get it up to his knees, but with a huge effort he managed it.

'Games at the Seashore' would have been the title of the scene that followed if I'd been a painter making a painting or a director making a short film. That's to say,

we two, surrounded by a horde of—I nearly said canni-
bals—first wet our feet in the shallows and then, splash-
ing about in the water, got our trousers soaked, and then
found flattish stones and played ducks and drakes. He
beat me, however hard I tried; you had to throw a stone
hard and make a whole series of bounces. We scrambled
up some nearby rocks and had a competition to see who
could get to the top first.

There was nothing special about what followed.
'Nothing to report', as military communiqués used to
put it during the war. The two of us had our fill of
playing in our own way in the water. Oh yes, there was
an accident: he trod on a sea urchin and got the spines
in his right foot. The sole of his foot was full of them,
so after that we decided to get out.

We dried in the sun and put our shoes and socks
back on. Soon the girls came back and complained again
that we hadn't joined them swimming, but they were
full of expressions of regret about the Café Sport man's
mishap with the sea urchin, and finally we all stretched
out to sunbathe.

It was a comic sight: two almost-naked girls, stretched
out on the sand, first on one side then on the other, and
the two men with them sitting in jackets and ties. Soon,
however, it became funnier still when one girl, his, having
fidgeted from side to side, announced:

'I must go for a pee, and you'll at least accompany me
for that! There are lots of men who annoy unaccompa-

nied girls; it's like that on these public beaches. And not just the public ones. Anyway, I hope you won't refuse.'

Our man looked at me like a fool.

'Can I ask you something?' I said to my girl. 'You don't happen to want to go for a pee, too, do you?'

She laughed.

'I hadn't thought about it,' she said, 'I mean, I didn't feel the need until now. But now you mention it, I'd be glad of the chance.'

So the problem was solved. I couldn't let him go that far away without me, of course. The toilets were at the other end of the beach, far away from where we were and from the bar where the third man had set himself up.

Soon the Café Sport man and I were standing double-guard outside the toilets, waiting. As for me, I had to hold my girl's bag—a huge straw bag, orange in colour. Very bright orange.

Then they went to the centre of the square to look at the fountain.

'It must be one of the sights of the town,' he said, 'judging by all the people sitting round and gazing at it, just like us.'

'The town doesn't have many monuments,' the Interrogator explained. 'Very few. You see, it's a fairly new town, apart from the harbour area. So, the fountain in the square... dammit, what's it called? Anyway, the fountain counts as a monument. The tourists come and take pictures. What else is there to take pictures of here?'

'Well anyway, it's a fine modern fountain. Imposing, but light at the same time. Abstract lines, carefully worked out details.'

'You should see it at night with the lights! It has amazing colours in unbelievable combinations.'

'At night? Oh, yes, you told me you'd been here before, twice.'

'Three times.'

'Our walk will certainly be over before they turn on the lights.'

The Interrogator took a small flat stone and threw it in the water.

'Yes, definitely over,' he said, making a gesture as if to confirm an unchangeable decision. 'Our walk will be over as soon as it gets dark. We agreed. Meanwhile we still have a little time; it's only 5.22.'

When they had left the square and fountain they decided to go to the other side of town, where they hadn't yet walked. It was the Interrogator's idea, but his companion had nothing against it.

'The neighbourhoods we're about to go through,' the Interrogator told him, 'have a quite different character to the centre of town. They're working-class areas, poor places, with roads no more than three metres wide, and generally...'

He stopped, as if thinking what to say next.

'There's no need to tell me more. I was born and passed my childhood years in just such a poor neighbourhood, I really enjoy wandering and getting lost in poor areas.'

Sometimes chatting, sometimes silent, they set out on their new wanderings.

'When I was a child I had lots of friends,' he told the Interrogator. 'We were a big crowd; we turned the place upside down with our shouting and running about. You've no idea the racket we made. You'd say the roads around our houses belonged to us exclusively; it was our own state.'

'I can't say the same for myself. I was a peaceful, well-behaved child. I liked to read—books, magazines, everything. Not just school books, I devoured whatever I could get my hands on. As a child I didn't bother with games.'

They were separated by a van which was suddenly upon them, going fast. One jumped one way, the other the other.

'It was coming straight at us!' said the Interrogator, 'As if he was aiming at us.'

They carried on walking.

'What was I saying? Ah, yes, the games in our neighbourhood. Once I remember we played hide-and-seek, and I went and hid in a basement warehouse, and the owner came, he had no idea I was inside, he locked it up thoroughly and went away on his bicycle. Until they found him and he came back swearing to let me out, what can I say, I was in a right state.'

'Now you're going to tell me you saw ghosts down there in the basement.'

'No, I didn't see any ghosts. But I saw something worse when I came out of my hiding place: my mother, come to get me. The other kids had told her and she'd run to get me out. As soon as I was safe and sound she gave me such a beating, it hurt as if she were slaughtering me; I can still feel it.'

The agent rubbed his nose.

'I feel for you,' he said. 'I've been beaten by my mother, too, so I understand what you're talking about.'

The afternoon was coming to its end; in half an hour or so it would be dark.

'Let's keep an eye on the time,' said the Café Sport man.

'I don't think we need to this time. When it gets dark we'll know, it will tell us it's time to go back to the Grand National.'

At that moment he saw the third man, of whom he'd lost trace for some time, following them at a distance. He wished he could wave at him, make some sign with his hands or his eyes.

'It was lovely at the seaside,' said the Café Sport man.

'You know, if things had been different, I'd have happily gone for an autumn swim.'

'Right up to the end our girls found it very strange that we refused to join them in the water.'

'Clearly I couldn't explain to them what was going on. But probably they accepted that we just didn't feel like swimming.'

'My girl—you probably noticed—gave me her number to ring her tomorrow afternoon. "Don't forget!" she said, and she mentioned it again several times. I didn't tell her that tomorrow we'll be a long way away.'

'Actually, I didn't ask you if maybe you would have liked to phone your girl—I mean the other girl, your girl in our town. You've been incommunicado ever since we left the Café Sport and she must be worried that you've disappeared.'

'No, my girl doesn't worry for the very good reason she doesn't exist. Lately I've been out of luck in that direction.'

He noticed that the agent gave him a very searching look, so he wondered, *Do they know I'm having an affair with her? No; if they had the slightest sign or information, they'd have said. Unless they're holding that card, and others perhaps, to play when we get to Central.*

An old man who could hardly put one foot in front of the other and had a little cardboard tray with chocolates, came up to them. His eyes looked deeply tired.

'Shall we buy some chocolate?' said the agent, stopping. 'How are things going, granddad? All well?'

'Bearing up, my boy. Sometimes I think I'm going to collapse, and sometimes I get the courage to carry on.'

'I felt sorry for the old man, too,' he said to the agent after they'd gone on their way. 'Every time I see little children, or little old ladies, or worn-out old men selling chocolates or whatever on the street or from café to café, getting chased away by the waiters as if they were flies, being chased by dogs...'

'Here, take your share. I hope the chocolate doesn't stick in your bad tooth.'

At the second corner they stopped at the mirror in a small shop—a tailor's—and combed their hair.

'My hair's all over the place from the wind,' said the agent.

'And mine. I'll have to do something about this dandruff, it's getting worse.'

'Oh, one has to look after one's hair. Don't you use a lotion?'

'No.'

'That's bad. I'll tell you what I use. I used to have dandruff, you wouldn't believe how persistent it was, but with this lotion it disappeared like magic within a week. Well, let's not exaggerate: it disappeared a month from the day I started using the lotion. Regularly, you see, morning and evening.'

And the Interrogator hurried along, still with the comb in his hand; he wanted to get the Café Sport man away from the mirror at once in, case he saw in the mirror the third man, standing ten metres away and feigning indifference. Because if our man had noticed him before he'd suspect that someone was following them.

When the ball came whizzing down from on high like a meteorite and bounced on the pavement just a metre to his right, the Interrogator's first thought was to leave it where it landed, and let one of the players come and get it. He saw it rolling towards a drain with half its grating broken away, and then he thought the player wouldn't get to it in time, and the ball, worn and patched as it was, would fall into the filthy water and rubbish of the drain. The only chance to save it was if he himself kicked it away. He didn't want to touch it with his hands, it was covered in dust and mud. But the Café Sport man got to it first and kicked it towards the playground. A bad shot; the ball stopped at the feet of the Interrogator. They exchanged a few passes, and meanwhile four or five of the players had run up and were joining in, passing the ball back and forth, and at one moment the Interrogator gave it a powerful kick that sent it into the net, right past the goalkeeper who was too late to stop it. The players and spectators broke into applause. The playing-field—an un-built-up space between some factories and the local cemetery, all covered in weeds and rubbish—was on fire with enthusiasm.

'Who would have thought you played such good football!' said the Café Sport man.

As if to show his skill, the agent feigned a kick without the ball and confessed:

'Between you and me, in all my thirty-five years, I doubt I've kicked a football more than five or six times. That kick I made that scored a goal was just luck: I aimed in one direction, the ball went in another.'

The players however were very excited and certainly hadn't guessed the secret. The Interrogator suddenly found himself surrounded by a crowd, of whom the tallest was one metre forty, one metre fifty at the most.

A little boy with his face all freckles shouted, 'I know him by his nose! And those great flappy ears like plane-tree leaves! Yes, that's him! The outside left from Lightning!'

'You don't know what you're talking about!' called another boy. 'He's the centre-half of Storm!'

'What are you saying!' insisted the first boy. 'I'll bet a packet of cigarettes he's the outside left from Lightning!'

There was practically a riot going on around him; the microscopic, unwashed, untidy, smudged-faced arguers were shoving each other to try and get the closest to him, to gawp at him, to talk to him. Eventually a thirteen-year-old with clumsily combed hair and a lame right leg managed to force his way through using his hands and his crutch, and took a packet of cigarettes out of the pocket of his jacket.

'Give me your autograph, mister!' he said, obviously very nervous. 'Don't say no!'

The Interrogator looked at him; the boy's big brown eyes were glued to him.

'OK!' he said. 'I'll make an exception just for you. I make it a rule not to give autographs, but I'll overlook that now.'

He took the packet and using the cheap ballpoint another boy gave him, he signed it.

At that point the referee blew his whistle for the game to continue, the match wasn't over yet, and the players ran off back to the pitch.

'What name did you put on the boy's cigarette packet?' the Café Sport man asked as they turned the corner.

'Not my own, for sure. While they were talking around me, one said I was the outside left of Lightning, another that no, I was the centre-half of Storm, and another I don't know what. I happened to hear the name of the centre-half of Storm, and I forged it.'

It didn't take me more than a second. I mean, no longer than I usually need to aim and pull the trigger. No, I didn't aim at his temple, or his heart, but at his mouth. There where his lips curved down to make that sarcastic smile of his, which made me want to hit him exactly there.

I got him, exactly on the smile. Well, I had no doubt that I would, I know what a good shot I am. As for him, he fell forward, not far, as if he were bowing or doing his morning exercises. And at the same moment, dozens of electric bells began ringing together and both the Café Sport man and I put our fingers in our ears so as not to be deafened.

'This prize is yours!' said the stall attendant officiously, giving me a large doll.

With justified pride, I took the award for my marksmanship. I'd give it to my wife; she has a great weakness for dolls.

The funfair was delaying our return to the Grand National; this is how it happened.

We'd finished with the football, and we decided to set out for the hotel. But we were in a dreadful state, all rumpled and dusty, as if we'd been in a fight.

'Let's at least get our shoes shined,' I said. 'I'm afraid that if we turned up at the hotel like this they'd throw us out on the street, or at least look down their noses at us.'

We asked around where we could get our shoes shined, and finally an old man told us that two blocks further down, on the right-hand corner, there was a little shop where they also shined shoes.

But it turned out we were fated not to return to the Grand National with shiny shoes, because as soon as we'd left the shoe-shine place and turned towards the centre of town, we found ourselves right by the funfair.

There was nothing very special about this local funfair, which had set itself up in a vacant building plot. Of course, it had all the usual funfair things, but it had something extra, something special which world-famous funfairs in the big capital cities don't have: it had a certain warmth, a friendly atmosphere well suited to the poor neighbourhood. It had a face, as it were; a face with strong masculine lines, rather dirty, like the faces of the people in this factory area, with children playing, turning somersaults in the dirt.

It was my idea to make this further extension to our walk—the very last, as I explained clearly!

'Ever since I was a child,' I told him, 'I don't know how to explain, but I feel a special charm in fairgrounds.'

'Really? I can't say the same for myself, but that's no reason we shouldn't go in for a while.'

We went to the entrance, which was decorated with flower-garlands and lots of coloured lights and little multi-coloured flags, just like a ship on a national holiday.

He beat me to the ticket counter.

'Ah, no!' I complained. 'You paid for the juices, I mean, my coffee and your juice. OK, we agreed about that as an exception, but in getting the tickets you're going too far!'

First, we did a 'ground reconnaisance'. We mingled in the crowd, and for all that it was Thursday, a working day, there were so many people you'd think it was a Sunday. We let the flow of the crowd take us where it would, just to get a taste of the place.

That little local fair had everything, as I think I said, for both children and adults. A puppet theatre, a doll-like little train which toured the place, full of passengers—and among them a few freeloading hangers-on. Two little ponies that took their job of taking children for rides very seriously. Lots of coin-operated machines where you could win or lose—mostly lose. Oh, yes, and the House of Mystery, which seemed to contain frightening things, judging from the faces of the people coming out. And there was a hall of distorting mirrors. And a whole row of shooting galleries... that was exactly where we joined in the fun of the fair: at a shooting gallery. You had to aim at a little man, ten centimetres high, which kept passing by with a sarcastic grin. But he went so fast it was very difficult to get him. He tried first and missed, then I took the gun myself. I aimed at the grin, the ironic grin. Got it first shot! That's when all the bells started ringing to congratulate me. And I took my prize oh so proudly: that very beautiful doll.

Then we went for a ride on the little train. The other chap, who was following us, went on foot, among many others doing the same. The train went very slowly and it was no problem to walk beside it; I saw him coming. I'd lost all track of him for some time; I'd been wondering if he was always close to us or if he, too, had lost track of us. The danger here in the fairground was the jostling crowd. The way the flow took us, it wouldn't be at all difficult for us to be swallowed up and for him to lose us. I confess there was no way I wanted to be alone in the fair with the Café Sport man. And anyway, I was tired enough from the journey, the long walk through the streets, and the football. Fortunately, the other agent was following us like a police dog, so I calmed down.

One could stay in the fair for hours and still find some new amusement. We, however, couldn't stay long.

But I kept postponing the decision to take him and leave. I was led astray by the whole atmosphere of the place, so many kinds of games, the lively rhythm, the hundreds of sightseers enjoying themselves with happy shouts and laughter, children, mothers, everyone. And of course, most of all I thought how this funfair atmosphere helped in the Plan; it would warm him up even more.

We went and looked at the puppet theatre. It was a very enjoyable programme, I laughed so much I had that pain in my stomach. He saw me doubling up and asked what was wrong, maybe I wasn't feeling well? No, I told him, I was feeling fine, it was just too much laughter. I didn't tell him about the stomach pain. I thought that if he knew it sometimes happened to me, it might increase his temptation to try to escape, and I'd prefer him not to try it here in the funfair. Even though the other man was following us closely, there was such a crowd of people it would be a great difficulty to catch him in time. And I didn't want to take the risk of managing the matter with the Café Sport man on my own. If he succeeded in getting away, no, it wouldn't be very pleasant. But just as I'd started to worry, I caught sight of the other man, nearer now, always following us despite the crowds.

'What are you going to do with the doll?' he asked me. 'Will you give it to your daughter, if she's young enough for it?'

We'd sat down at the bar—one of three or four at various points in the fairground—and ordered, not juice or coffee this time, but beer. Beer doesn't contain much alcohol.

'No, my daughter's not so little, for the simple reason I don't have a daughter. We don't have any children yet.'

'I didn't know.'

'We decided not to, for now. Not for very long. First I wanted to make sure of my position in the Special Branch. I mean, to get a raise, which I hope to soon. And you, when do you plan to have a family? I know you're not married; I know quite a lot about you, why should I hide it?'

'Yes, I thought you did. You and the Manager. Anyway, none of that's a secret. But no, I haven't thought of marriage yet.'

'Don't tell me that your first thought when we get back from the capital will be marriage?'

We laughed then, and a woman at a nearby table who was drinking a lemon granita with a straw was infected by it and started laughing herself without knowing why.

'Back in two minutes! How many copies would you like, two? One each?'

I hadn't noticed the street photographer, who'd quickly snapped a picture of us as we were laughing. If I'd noticed him while he was taking our picture, I'd have chased him off. An agent of the Special Branch should stay in the shadows, incognito: he's not like other people who are free to have their picture taken in public places, like fairgrounds. But now that he'd taken the picture I was going to tell him no, we didn't want any copies, but the Café Sport man got in first, took out some money and paid him in advance.

'Let me treat you to the photographs,' he said, 'as a souvenir of our stroll through the town.'

He seemed so moved by the idea—was he making a fool of me?—that I let him. Anyway, I thought this little detail of having our picture taken together in the fairground would be good for the Plan.

'You keep getting up to things!' I told him.

And I really did find it amusing when the photographer came back with the pictures, my pose was so funny, with my beer-glass raised as if proposing a toast and with an idiotic expression of laughter.

We each took our copy. I put mine in my wallet, and he put his in an inside pocket of his jacket.

'If I try to put it in my wallet it will get all crumpled,' he said, 'and I don't want that.'

It was a long time since I'd been to a funfair, maybe five or six years. And now I had the chance—and a chance that went so well with the Plan—to live again the intense, special happiness that the fairground atmosphere brought me. And it could all be part of the Plan.

There was hardly a game we didn't try. I had a thirst—we had a thirst—to try everything, all the entertainments offered by that warm friendly fair. For sure, time was up; it was already dark. Maybe we should have left earlier, but I let us stay a little longer, the temptation was too great. Anyway, it wouldn't have been easy for him to escape. The other man was always near, I'd see him from time to time, then I'd lose him again. I knew he was following us, pretending to watch some sideshow or a game of roulette.

Something we enjoyed very much was the hall of distorting mirrors, which was quite an unusual, strange show. I'd never seen anything like it before. I'd happened to see my face in distorting mirrors once or twice; some shops put such mirrors near the entrance by the window, to attract customers. But it was the first time I'd been in an entire room—and with various little rooms adjoining—completely surrounded by a whole collection of distorting mirrors. My eyes, my ears, my lips, my hands looked so strange, so monstrous, unnatural, absurd. And of course, with the Café Sport man right beside me, our faces were sometimes confused one with the other, as if one merged into the other.

We left the House of Mystery until last in our exploration of the fun-fair. This was a very old house with three floors, which at one time had been a tobacco warehouse before it had been abandoned. They told us all about it as we were waiting to get our tickets to enter the House of Mystery it had now become.

When the funfair came to set itself up in that area, they found the house abandoned, this one-time tobacco warehouse, and very cleverly the fairground managers had transformed it into the House of Mystery.

It wasn't the first time I'd been in a House of Mystery, and the Café Sport man said he, too, had been in one once or twice. But each such place has its own mystery. And it was with longing and curiosity, and even a little fear, just as if I were a child, that I waited for the tickets that let us cross the threshold.

The first thing we saw when we went in was that we didn't in fact see anything at all. It was so dark that I confess I felt rather uneasy. Not, of course, because any-thing bad might happen to us in the House of Mystery, but rather that he might get away from me in the pitch blackness. I had my torch with me, on my key-ring, a microscopic but powerful torch. But I wouldn't be able to do much with just a torch. The House of Mystery was all twists and turns, and if he wanted to try and get away... it was stupid of me, very risky, to suggest that we visit this dark building.

We travelled on to a point where there wasn't the slightest glimmer of light.

Yes, but there was one security: the other man. He didn't come into the House of Mystery; it was the only time he didn't follow us. I saw him, while the Café Sport man and I were queuing for our tickets; he wasn't in the queue but walking a few steps away. He gave me a look as if to say, 'I shall wait for you here, in front of the entrance.' It was better that way, because if anything happened to me in the House of Mystery, if our man got away from me, at least we had the guarantee that the other one would catch him when he came out.

The only light—and that only for seconds—came from the kind of sudden flashes that would have kept one awake all night. Doors opened and closed with such force and noise that we might have been at the centre of a hurricane; nightmarish shadows appeared every now and then for a second and then would suddenly disappear into the darkness like ghosts, pistol shots and strangled human voices rang out, dogs howled as if only a couple of metres away. There were explosions sometimes to the left of us, sometimes to the right, a roaring wind that lifted us off our feet like toys so that we could hardly stand upright and had to cling to the walls to go from room to room, from floor to floor, from surprise to surprise.

I thought it was yet another surprise when the music suddenly stopped. Yes, the House of Mystery had music, too; maybe I should have said so before. Loudspeakers placed at suitable points played appropriate music, something like the soundtrack in a thriller.

From the moment we set foot in the House of Mystery this music accompanied us step by step, colouring and underlining, sometimes obviously and sometimes more subtly, each surprise along the way.

Well, I thought this sudden cut in the music, which had been playing continuously up to then, was just a short break, done deliberately to emphasise the Grand Guignol atmosphere, or perhaps a break in the tape. The interval didn't last long, less than a minute. But afterwards we didn't have music again, but a voice much amplified by the loudspeakers, which could be heard right through the whole place:

'Our respected visitors are asked to go at once to the exit! A crack has just been discovered in the building, and there is a serious and immediate danger that it will collapse.'

The first reaction was silence. And immediately after, sporadic laughter, chiefly from a group of women— short, sharp laughter.

'Not such a clever trick!' said someone, it was impossible to see who in the darkness.

'If you had a weak heart, you might have a heart attack,' someone else added.

'That's saying too much, my friend,' the first voice— probably—continued. 'Things aren't that tragic. After all, we're in a House of Mystery; what d'you expect? It's all part of the game.'

'Keep calm!' said the loudspeakers again, 'Proceed in an orderly manner to the exit.'

No, I don't want to pretend to be clever and say I knew what was happening. I had the same idea as the others in the group—there were about ten or eleven of us, I'd counted quickly as we went in—I, too, had the idea it was a trick. How was I to guess that everything wasn't as it should be?

There was a second burst of laughter after the second announcement, but our optimism didn't last long. There was an underground roar, something between an earthquake and a dynamite explosion, and then a strong wind howled around us; all this in the impenetrable darkness was too much for us to take. In a second, a spark of panic set fire to us all.

'It's not a trick!' I heard from beside me. 'But where's the way out?'

Finding the exit was indeed the problem: the flashes of light during the first part of our journey, which had at least let us find our way through the labyrinth, weren't there anymore and we were in total darkness. We all huddled together, turning now right, now left, trying to get out of this mousetrap before the House of Mystery collapsed on top of us in a cataract of rotten wood, earth and rocks.

'I can't breathe!' Our man told me. 'Something's pressing on my chest.'

The second time he spoke to me I was reassured that he was still near me. This chaos and darkness was an opportunity for him to escape, in spite of the fact that there was someone waiting for him outside the House of Mystery.

'Last warning!' came the voice from the loudspeakers. 'Visitors should not in any circumstances delay in hurrying to the exit. The crack is widening and visitors must understand the immediate danger.'

The children in our group began to cry, and the women, too, I think; strange noises surrounded us. We ten or eleven were frantic, and everything we said echoed—the House of Mystery had a very marked echo—as if picked up by an invisible amplifier and relayed back to us in stereo. How could we guess if we were really heading for the way out or just going round in circles?

'I'm afraid we're never going to get out of here,' said our man as he took my hand. 'Is that *your* hand?'

'As it happens, yes. It might not have been.'

Now the two of us continued hand in hand, like two children lost in a dark forest.

'Just in case our visit to the House of Mystery has no sequel,' he whispered to me, 'I want you to know that our excursion has been very enjoyable, and I thank you.'

I felt his warm breath on me and, I don't know, just for a second, only a second, I felt a lump in my throat. I couldn't say why; a strange lump in my throat.

'Attention! Visitors are informed that they have now arrived at the exit. Forgive us for the trick we played!'

And then there was a bright light, ahead and to the right, but not from an explosion: floodlights bathed us in a light so strong I had to put my hand in front of my eyes.

'Can I take your pillow, too?' I asked him, 'Unless of course you want to lie down now.'

He was standing in front of one of the three pictures in room 717. There was one on each wall except the wall with the window.

'Go ahead. No, I don't feel at all like lying down, not yet anyway.'

I put the pillows upright against the bedhead; two for my back and a third for my head; I'd taken the Manager's, too, his bed being empty. And I pulled a chair over to the foot of the bed so as not to dirty the sheets with my shoes.

'I thought you wanted to lie down properly but to have your head a bit higher.'

'No, I just wanted to do just as you see. From childhood I've liked to sit on the bed propped up against the bedhead; I find it relaxing.'

I saw him stand and stare at the picture; a reproduction that was somehow familiar, though it didn't remind me of anything in particular. A young woman getting out of the bath and putting her slippers on.

'Shame on you, staring like that!' I teased him. 'You're putting the girl in a difficult position.'

'She's got a mole on her right breast.'

'Bravo! I had no idea you had such good eyesight.'

'When it comes to breasts, yes I do. The first thing that catches my eye in a woman is her breasts. They have a certain charm for me, something I can't express. When I caress them, lick them, bite them...'

'Who's the picture by?'

'There's a mark here but I can't make it out. Well, our walk in the town was quite some walk!'

And he brushed away the ash from his cigarette where it had fallen on his jacket.

'Whose idea was it, I'd like to know! Don't I deserve congratulations for it?'

He laughed and was about to say something, but then he bent to tie his right shoelace.

'I don't understand what it is about this lace, it keeps coming undone. And yesterday in the Café Sport...'

'I'm still waiting for the congratulations' I said.

'Oh yes! It was an excellent idea of yours, that walk in the town. We stretched our legs, saw and heard lots of things. And we found really good company and went down to the sea, breathed in the sea air, a little sunbathing—and we played football. We had a good time at the fair, shared the danger in the House of Mystery—in short, we had a really nice time.'

He took the other chair and sat at the little table. 'I'm going to try the crossword,' he said, opening the *Evening News*.

'If you need any help, just ask.'

'Right; if I get stuck.'

Everything had gone not just well, but perfectly. The Plan, the whole scheme, had gone like clockwork. Now all they had to do was wait for results. They set a time-bomb which would definitely go off, at some as-yet-unknown time.

He felt that the Plan was a living thing, a creature with nerves and movement, and the two of them had worked together towards a common end. The Plan had entered his blood, become part of him. He and the Plan were one entity. In the beginning, when the Chief had revealed the Plan, yes, he'd accepted it at once, but mostly with his mind, not with his heart. He hadn't fully warmed to it. They had to get to know each other slowly, the Plan and its operator. To get mixed up in this improbable adventure, which had begun that morning at seven, 550 kilometres away, in the inner courtyard at Special Branch, and secretly they'd moved it along, with the greatest care, like two co-conspirators. The Plan and the Interrogator: two co-conspirators.

Of course, it was dangerous, acting a part, pretending to be a normal person who had what they call 'feelings'. If they'd asked him to subject the Café Sport man to intense interrogation, to interrogate him unfeelingly for hours, forever, if they'd asked him to do something like that, yes. But to put on a mask, to play the part of a normal person, was to enter an entirely new country, which he didn't know, where he'd never been before. Now this new unknown thing had won him over. It was like going about in virgin territory, exploring it bit by bit. The Plan had the piquant charm of danger.

In my seven years as an interrogator with the Special Branch, this is the first time I have had to pretend to be someone other than myself.

If only I had a mirror! A pocket mirror to hold during all the time I was playing my part, to have it in front of my false face, opposite my false eyes, to follow, moment by moment, my expression, according to the particular circumstances of the Plan as it proceeded.

I watched him out of the corner of my eye as he tried to solve his crossword. Did he suspect? But how to suspect a Plan such as this one, which had nothing special or strange about it, a Plan that worked gently, imperceptibly? As if one were talking calmly with friends, and a knife went into your guts with such skill that you didn't even notice what was happening until the moment you fell to the ground.

'Can I ask you something?' he said to him. 'I've been struggling for ages with this four down.'

'At last! I'm very pleased you want my help. What's the clue? Famous courtesan of ancient times? Romantic composer of the eighteenth century?'

'No,' he said, laughing, 'neither of those. Four down, and I can't work out what it is, is this: "River that not only drowns but devours."'

'"River that not only drowns but devours."'

'You're my only hope. You know how long I've been stuck on this mysterious man-eating river?'

'Strange! I can't think of anything. Search me! And I'm proud of being such an ace at crosswords.'

'Well, don't give yourself a headache. I think I'll leave four down for the moment and look at the across clues. Later I can try again.'

'Fine. You carry on, and I'll try and figure out which is this miraculous river.'

When the agent had offered to help him as he bent over the *Evening News*, he was pretending to think only of the crossword but in fact his mind was on something else. Yes, he'd definitely lost the game. From the moment they'd come back to room 717, from the moment they'd crossed the threshold and he heard and saw the key turn twice—two dry and definite sounds, like pistol shots—from that second, everything inside him, his thoughts, his heart, his guts, the microorganisms in his body, his intuition, everything had fallen into a tightly closed dark night. He had no hope now! He'd played all his cards. No, he hadn't played any cards at all. He'd just stood uselessly by throughout the unique opportunity of the walk in town, unable to do anything or react to anything. As if they'd given him a woman whom he strongly desired, and he'd lain next to her naked and willing body and had been quite impotent.

In the glass of the window, he saw his own face, dull, cloudy, seeming to be etched on the glass. He felt a wave of disgust and spat forcefully at the face in the glass. Then immediately he took out his handkerchief and wiped his spit away.

'What's the matter?' asked the Interrogator.

'Mosquito! Instead of hitting it with my hand, I had the idea of spitting at it, but I missed.'

'I don't think it matters if there are mosquitos in the room. We're unlikely to sleep; at five or a little before the Manager will come with the car.'

'That's right. No sleep tonight.'

He pretended to be busy with his crossword again. How had he let such an opportunity slip through his fingers! The reason was fear: fear, which suddenly penetrated and bit his heart, gnawing at it ceaselessly, the fear that all this was play-acting whose only aim was to make him fall into the trap. To make him want to escape, and so show that he was guilty. Special Branch had nothing on him. That's what this was about. If he didn't keep calm, he himself would prove his own guilt. If he was provoked into making a run for it, that would be the knife that his own hand would stab into his heart. Ah, no! That was just what the Special Branch were counting on. So he shouldn't play their game. The moment he'd run to escape, the Special Branch agent wouldn't stand there and admire him. He'd shoot him, aiming at his legs to get him alive. His attempt to escape would be a clear confession. Yes, there was also the possibility he'd succeed. But what possibility? And could he risk taking that tiny chance, having before him the many chances of falling into their hands a second time, injured, or that they might find him later, when the whole machinery of Special Branch was set into motion. And even if he got away, would he manage to get in touch with his own people so that they could hide him, get him a false identity card and passport, so that they could get him over the border? All very doubtful. And then, suppose the other Café Sport man hadn't in fact been arrested but had got away, and the Chief was bluffing, pretending they'd caught him? And even if they had caught the other man, how could he be sure that he'd in fact confessed? And if he hadn't confessed, if he'd thrown dust in their eyes, and the face-to-face interrogation they were planning came to nothing? There was also the possibility that Special Branch wasn't playing a game at all and everything was straightforward, so that if he tried to get away he would again fall into the trap, he himself showing them he was guilty.

When they were travelling in the car: and all through the walk in town, there was an ebb and flow of thoughts in his head. Sometimes it flowed in the direction of escape, sometimes towards fear and doubt. Perhaps his attempt to escape would fail and he would fall again into the hands of the Special Branch...

But now it was very late and harder to think of what to do. In room 717 of the Grand National, past midnight, with the door double-bolted and the Special Branch agent wide awake, his pistol ready to do its own talking, was it or was it not too late now? The subject was closed. All he had to wait for now was the Manager to come back with the car at five, and they would leave on the ferry, and then they would hand him over to Central. And there, what had he to expect? A dark dead end waited for him in the capital, a total dead end without hope.

'I've still got half the crossword to do,' he said. 'And of course, there's still that mysterious river which "not only drowns but devours".'

'Oh, we'll discover that river,' I assured him. 'It's a matter of inspiration. The word will come to us just when we're not looking for it.'

If only it were possible to guess the mysterious workings going on inside him! How the Plan had worked on his organism, how it had slowly soaked into him, and what the result would be.

The only thing I knew well, that I was sure of, was that I'd given all my abilities to the Plan. A very simple Plan in its conception, its idea, but very difficult in its operation. One single detail could wipe out all our efforts. I understood how difficult it was when we started to put the theory into practice. The Café Sport man was no fool. The worst would be to underestimate his resistance or to overestimate one's powers. No, he wasn't stupid. And of course, if he was guilty, then his thoughts, his perceptions, his intuitions, would be especially sharp.

Fortunately, everything—as far as I could see myself—had gone well. Now, were getting to the end of the story: the night wore on and in a few hours the Manager would be knocking at the door. We still had the ferry trip and the drive to the capital. The main thing however, the basic part of the Plan, had been completed: the walk in town.

I got up from the bed to relieve my numbness. I stretched my arms.

'How's the crossword going?' I asked him.

'I don't know. I'm tired and dizzy, or not on form, or maybe it's an especially difficult crossword. I'm not too satisfied. Anyway, I hope to finish it before the Manager comes.'

'The Manager will be late; he made it clear to us that there was no question of his coming before five.'

I started to look at the pictures on the walls, beginning with the one on the wall next to the bathroom.

This *Spring Sea* had what they call atmosphere, personality, even though the subject wasn't original, I thought. Was the 'subject' of the Plan original? A walk in town... A very common theme, but with its special circumstances it had its own personality. It was the Special Branch's Plan, yes, but in its operation it had taken on the personality we two gave it, the Café Sport man and myself. Two people working together on the Plan, one with full will and knowledge, the other unsuspecting.

However, I couldn't guess or foresee how it might continue. What was going to happen in the end, and how soon it would happen. How to know the extent, and the depth to which the Plan had eaten him away, or would eat him away? I was in the dark. I'd run an experiment and was waiting for the result. There were no marks or indications to show me its impact. The Café Sport man was opposite me, in front of the closed window, smoking, bent over his crossword. I hadn't spotted anything remarkable about him during all the time we'd been together. Nothing that would let me diagnose what had happened inside him, if the Plan had hooked him or not.

'Since you're concentrating on the crossword, could you give me the rest of the paper to look at?'

He tore out the page with the crossword and gave him the rest. Then the Interrogator drew a chair nearer to the table and sat down.

'I suggest we put one of the bedside lights here, to see better. You with your crossword, me with the newspaper. That overhead light doesn't seem very strong to me.'

'What could be easier?' he said obligingly. 'So long as the cable is long enough.'

He brought the lamp from his own bedside table, and fortunately the cable wasn't only long enough, but reached the opposite corner of the table.

'Now we're fine!' said the Interrogator gratefully, and buried himself in the *Evening News*.

While seeming busy with the crossword, he let his thoughts return to the same theme. What was the point of thinking it through over and over again? There was no more room for anything; time was against him, every minute that passed, every second, was against him. His watch said 1.22. If the Manager finished before five, all three of the group could soon be in 717. But even now, with just the two of them, the situation was hopeless. He could see out of the corner of his eye that the man was reading the newspaper, he could hear his breath, he could feel the Special Branch agent next to him, ready to draw his pistol... like a gust of wind, the thought occurred to him to pounce on the agent that very second, to struggle with him, to hit him with all his might mercilessly! But no, he didn't do it. Fear had glued him to his chair; again he felt contempt for himself, disgust.

With what certainty he'd started out that morning! Right at the start, when they got in the car, the Manager's suggestion that they should all sit together in the front seat gave him a flash of hope; he hoped he'd find an opportunity during the journey to wipe out both his guards at the same time. The Manager's idea gave him a big advantage! Two well-aimed punches at the same time, one for the Manager and one for the other to his right, and he'd be away! And indeed, he'd started to work out the details. First of all, where did they keep their pistols? In the Manager's case, he knew. When they were setting out from the inner courtyard, the Manager had lifted the bonnet for a moment and bent down over it, and then he saw the pistol in the back pocket of his trousers. But he didn't know where the other one had his. It would be a valuable piece of information. When he threw those two punches, one to the left and one to the right, he needed to know what movement each of them would make to grab their pistols. It didn't take him long to find out. When the Manager said he'd been a manager of fleas, he had the inspired idea of pretending that he itched whenever he heard the word 'flea', and as he scratched himself he leant against the other man. Then he felt the pistol in the man's inside left jacket pocket. He managed the pretend itch so well that it was impossible they suspected anything. Yes, now he had the information he needed. As they were going along at 110 kilometres an hour, his imagination turned to a scene in a thriller—or was it a cowboy film?—where he'd seen something just like that: the hero was being taken somewhere in a car by two baddies when suddenly he dealt two punches like dynamite, one left and one right, as the car was doing 150 kilometres an hour—in the film it was 150, not 110— which pushed both his guards out into the road, completely dazed by the sudden attack, and our hero grabbed the wheel. Something like that—exactly like that—he would do at the right moment, just as the film hero dared to do and succeeded . Yes, it was a cowboy film, a western. He was very pleased he'd remembered that film. In a little while, however, he began to have doubts; had he really seen such a film, with such a scene, or was it a fantasy, now that they were going along at 110?

But he must get away from them at all costs! He must exploit everything: the tiredness that the two agents must be feeling from the long journey, the relative exhaustion from the heat, this debilitating sultriness; he must exploit the opportunity of the moment, even exploit—especially exploit—the fact that they happened to be simple people, almost idiots, these two agents he was travelling with. Yes, that was a very important fact! It would help him a lot in his attempt to get away, an attempt that must come off! He must certainly exploit their friendly behaviour towards him, talking to him as if nothing had happened, their easy conversation—generally, the fact that they weren't the serious, silent, unsmiling types to whom one couldn't get close, and, naturally, couldn't fool by playing the innocent. So on the car journey with the two agents, he had started to play the same part he'd played when they arrested him in the the Café Sport—pretending that he was innocent, that he was so innocent as to not even be worried or anxious about anything, he was simply naturally and quite justifiably annoyed that the ordeal was dragging on so long. He didn't go to the other extreme of pretending that it didn't bother him at all that they were taking him to Central, 910 kilometres from their town. The correct, the really intelligent tactic was to show at the same time both annoyance and calm, since he pretended to have faith that the people he'd be handed over to at Central would comprehend at once that he wasn't guilty, that he wasn't in any way mixed up in organisations working against the Regime, and they'd set him free at once, the very evening when they'd arrive at Central. He took that position from the start, giving the impression that he wasn't worried about the outcome, just that when they would get to Central the matter would be sorted out and they'd let him go. Yet, he was in an agony of fear that there, at Central, everything would be over for him. The least he would have to endure would be an interrogation, not with the velvet gloves and easy manner used—deliberately?—by the Chief, but the kind of interrogation that only the Special Branch would know how to carry out.

While they were travelling in the car, he started conversations at every opportunity the two gave him, or created opportunities himself so as to maintain the friendly atmosphere. He knew nothing about the two agents, but he had no doubt that they knew everything or at least a lot about him and the Café Sport story. The Chief would certainly have informed them, or they would themselves have asked. But what should he ask his two guards? And then he was afraid they might find his interest suspicious. Anyway, what was the point? Well, no, that sort of conversation would strengthen the warmth that already existed. As to the Manager, he'd already discovered during the journey that he had been a manager in wrestling matches. About the other he hadn't dared to ask anything, and nothing had come up in conversation; later, maybe. Anyway, he had to deal with two Special Branch agents, nothing more nor less. Two determined, merciless agents, who under their friendly or apparently friendly manner, their smiles and chewing gum, hid two hearts and pistols of steel. He'd have to work out perfectly the escape attempt he would make at the right moment. He knew what would happen if it went wrong.

The 110 kilometres an hour they'd been doing the whole way was bringing them closer and closer to the harbour and the ferry. He'd been telling them the truth when he'd said that all his previous trips to the capital had been by rail; he'd never before been by

car and ferry. If he had, he'd have told them so. He would-
n't let them catch him lying about such a minor matter
and make his position even more difficult.

But bit by bit he realised that his planned escape
would be no easy matter. The scene he'd watched in the
film—if he really had—couldn't be repeated second by
second. He began to doubt whether he could really
manage it. Then suddenly came the first delay, with the
Manager and the other man worrying that there was
something wrong with the engine. As before, with the
traffic jam at the junction of National Route 37 and National Route 40, and the conversation they'd had about
rain, he pretended that all he was worried about was
whether they'd make it to the capital and to Central
that same day. But then his thoughts became troubled:
suppose by good luck something went wrong and the
journey was delayed... surely such a delay would be to
his advantage. But the Manager didn't find anything
wrong in particular, and he was disappointed to see him
get back in the car and start the engine. But later, at
kilometre 214 on National Route 40, there really was an
engine problem. He could hardly keep himself from
shouting, 'Hurray!' or, 'Well done, distributor!' But he
should take care not to give himself away; now was precisely the time to keep cool. What next? To begin with,
they'd missed the ferry and would have to stay overnight
in town so as to catch the 6.20 ferry in the morning.
Where would they take him to pass the night? In a cell

at the local Special Branch? Somewhere else? But where? A hotel? Surely not. But if it really was a hotel, then lots of possibilities presented themselves.

Now that I was here alone in room 717 of the Grand National, with the Café Sport man trying to solve his crossword, or perhaps doing nothing of the sort but thinking about other matters, or not thinking at all, but as far as appearances went, he was deep in his crossword. Well, now that I was peacefully settled in room 717 and was sorting out my impressions of how the Plan was going so far, I realised how right the Chief had been when he'd said, 'The Plan is a work of genius!' and 'Astonishing!' Certainly, I still didn't have any particular proof for all that I felt about it, but I was sure that's how it was. My intuition—in which I always have blind faith—assured me that the Plan had entered deeply into our man and was working in him secretly towards the result we wanted: his final breakdown, thanks to the humane, very humane, means we had used in accordance with the Plan. I didn't have the slightest doubt that the Plan had hooked our man; our man who was the pipe we had subjected to sudden changes of temperature, the guinea-pig on whom we had practiced the inspired experiment that was the Plan. Ah, if only I could shake hands with the creator of the Plan! If I could just run up to him and shake him by the hand! It would be difficult if the creative genius of the Plan turned out to be an electronic brain. But there would be a solution: a button to push to express the warm enthusiasm I felt for its creativity, for the astonishing Plan, to show my respect and joy, my emotion, that I was the first to put it into operation.

Well, intuition is a very interesting, very special thing. I didn't have any tangible proof that the Plan had worked, not even an indication, but I was one hundred percent certain that at any moment, maybe here and now in room 717 of the Grand National, maybe later on the rest of our journey to the capital, maybe at Central where our man would again suddenly be subjected to a different temperature—incredibly icy—I was one hundred percent certain that the pipe, the guinea-pig, would finally break. He would confess.

As for me, and my part in running the Plan, I'd given it my all. Both with my mind and my instincts, I'd gone ahead with the utmost care, and had not done the tiniest thing that could upset the Plan; I hadn't neglected the slightest detail necessary for the Plan to work.

From the time we'd set out in the car, I'd created this human, this simple everyday human situation which the Plan required. Certainly the Manager had helped me a lot.

And here and now, in the meditative atmosphere of room 717, I gathered together all the details—well, not all of them, that would be impossible. But most of them. Or rather, many. For example, my pretence of emotion, my near silliness about nature, about the beauties of nature and country life, and the repartee I'd had with the Manager, who'd understood at once and had cleverly taken the opposite point of view, that he wasn't like me, setting up a contrast which would be of use to us in time.

And then, later, when I dashed out of the car when we were stuck at the crossroads for National Route 40 and gathered wildflowers. I arranged my bouquet on the dashboard, and, best of all, our man helped me. Then I gave him a little mauve flower to put in his buttonhole. So all that, which in other circumstances I would never have done, and I'd have been furious if I'd seen another person doing, I did for the sake of the Plan, putting on a mask and playing a part.

How can I concentrate right now on all these details which, bit by bit, as we were going along at 110, were weaving together into the Plan? Apparently friendly, heart-felt conversations, glances of pretended sympathy, smiles, in brief, a homely atmosphere but not overdone so that the Café Sport man could breathe more easily, warm up little by little, become more open, up to the time that he'd break.

Wasn't it just perfect, that scene with the faulty distributor? Both the first and the second time we stopped. The Manager and I played our parts with incredible naturalness, as if there'd really been something wrong and we were driven crazy missing the ferry and not getting to Central the same day. When I bring to mind the moment that creep the motorcycle policeman turned up, I can feel again the shiver it brought. Things nearly went badly wrong there; it would have ruined the whole Plan. And why? For nothing! Luckily we got away with it at the last moment. But if that unexpected and oh-so-helpful policeman had just come a half metre closer and had bent over the open bonnet, discovered that the distributor was perfectly all right and shouted, 'There's nothing wrong with it, you're making it up!' that would have been a catastrophe.

'How's the crossword going?' asked the Interrogator, who'd probably finished the newspaper or got bored with it.

'I've still got lots of words to go; I'm not on form this evening.'

'And how about that "river that not only drowns but devours"? Did you work it out?'

He shook his head and said, 'Just now I felt like abandoning this crossword. But I'll keep trying. Out of stubbornness, and to pass the time.'

The Interrogator got up, leaving the *Evening News* at the foot of the bed. He went to the door, got out the key and tried it in the lock.

'I don't know how I got the idea,' he said as if to himself, 'But I thought I didn't lock it when we came in.'

He went back to his chair and picked up the paper again, and said something under his breath that the Café

Sport man couldn't hear. Anyway, the latter was drawn again into a maelstrom of doubts and questions. How could he have left such a golden opportunity unexploited! But, in fact, from the moment he'd learnt that they were going to Central, and even more so from the time they'd got stuck because of the distributor, he'd been lifted on a wave of optimism. He was completely given over to his longing to escape. On the journey, as they were hurrying for the ferry, and later when they were walking to the town, there wouldn't have been a chance. He would have to wait until they got to the hotel, when he'd have time until tomorrow morning when they left for the ferry. It was enough that they'd in the end gone to a hotel and he hadn't been left at the local Special Branch. It was impossible that there'd be no opening, no break in his imprisonment. Then, like lightning, he'd be through it and away.

In the telephone box at the petrol station, when they told him to get in with them, he'd pretended not to be very interested in their conversation with the Chief. Not as if he'd been completely indifferent; total indifference would have been unnatural and they'd have thought it suspicious. He'd had to struggle not to show his enthusiasm when he heard the Chief talking about a hotel. It was exactly what he wanted! But how uneasy he'd been later, in Railway Station Square, while they were waiting for the Manager to find a room. If there didn't happen to be a hotel room of the sort the Special

Branch men wanted, then faced with that impossibility, they'd have had to take him to a cell at the local Special Branch. Luckily a suitable room turned up, and with the advantage of a window overlooking the courtyard. He quickly considered the width of the ledge. Not very wide, but wide enough to walk on very carefully until he got to the outside service stairs and so down to the street... When would the time come for that! He'd have to wait for the Manager to leave first, and then when he was alone with the other man he'd jump on him and play for all he had!

Then there was the wait for the Manager's phone call from the workshop. The first call came. A little later, the second. He didn't want to try it until the phone calls were over. If he knocked him out and then the Manager phoned and got no answer, it would complicate matters.

While they were playing chess, his thoughts were on the desperate move he'd soon make to knock out the Special Branch man. *Some moment when his attention is on something else, I'll land a punch on his face, right between the eyes!* But he changed his mind when the agent wanted to go to the toilet. Then, as he waited outside the toilet, singing the national anthem, he'd been astonished to hear the agent's sudden suggestion that the two of them go for a walk in town. It was the best thing that could possibly have happened! But he hid his astonishment and even seemed doubtful about the idea, but not too doubtful in case the other should change his mind and withdraw the suggestion.

After the fake distributor problem, the rest came 'naturally'. We did what anyone else would do who had the same difficulty. Since our attempts to hitchhike or catch a bus didn't succeed, we started walking. We'd foreseen everything, in accordance with the Plan. If someone stopped for us, we'd get in only if he took all three of us. And we'd take a bus only if there were three seats, otherwise no.

At the petrol station we told him—the Manager told him—to get in the phone box with us. As if we weren't bothered that he'd hear the phone call with the Chief. Oh, yes, the Manager took the initiative many times, and not just by chance. We'd thought it all out before, so that it would seem we were just the same: two simple agents.

There was no possibility the Chief wouldn't be available when we rang. We'd worked out the time to call him with the greatest precision, and he'd be waiting for us, but we pretended to be afraid we might not find him in. As for the conversation, it would have fooled even the most suspicious. Both the Manager and the Chief played their parts perfectly. I was slyly looking at the Café Sport man in the phone box, and I could see that he'd pricked up his ears so as not to miss a word, and anyway, the Chief could be heard clearly.

Then, in accordance with instructions from the Chief—as if given to us for the first time then and there—we had to look for a hotel, so as not to involve the local Special Branch. So we carried on trudging towards town.

On the road, we stopped a while to draw lots and see which of us would stay with our man and which would go to the repair shop. I took four pebbles in my right hand and asked the Manager to guess even or odd. If he got it right, he'd be the one to wait in the hotel, and if not, he'd have all the fuss of the repair shop. 'Odd!' said the Manager after pretending to think about it. 'You've lost!' I told him. How could our man guess that we'd agreed the night before that he should say, 'Odd!'?

The Manager's searching for a hotel room that was just right—three beds, its own bathroom, not on the ground floor—was another farce we played. We two waited in Station Square while the Manager went from one hotel to another without finding such a room, then finally found one at the Grand National: room 717, which the Chief had taken care to reserve. The Manager hadn't asked for a room at all at the other hotels.

Everything had gone according to the Plan. The Manager left us in room 717 as soon as he'd drunk his orangeade, so hurriedly that he'd spilt some on the floor—by chance or had he done it deliberately for emphasis? Anyway, he left us and went to find a workshop to see to the 'repair'.

At first we in room 717 played chess. In the meantime, the Manager phoned twice and I made a fuss when he told us the repair would take until about five in the morning so that I'd have to stay shut up in 717 with our man all night.

Then came the time for me to tell him about our walk in the town. The third agent was already waiting for us in the Six Fingers bar. When we came out, he'd follow us unobserved. In any case, an extra pistol is always useful. Yes, I knew that the other man was already in the bar, that he'd traveled up from our town just like us, according to the Plan. If anything had gone wrong, such as his being delayed and not reaching the bar, then when the Manager made his first call he wouldn't have told me that he was already at the workshop arranging the towing of the car, so I would have known and wouldn't have hurried to say anything about our walk. But everything was all right. I had to make the suggestion about the walk very carefully, not as if I were overly keen on the idea, not insistently, and then give up the idea if he didn't feel like it or thought it boring, or he was tired. I had to suggest the idea as if it had been a flash of inspiration. A walk in town: not a long one—say, an hour. I had to serve the idea up to the Café Sport man so that he wouldn't have the slightest suspicion anything was hidden behind such an innocent suggestion. Not provoking any resistance that might make him refuse, suspecting some hidden plan.

Fortunately, he fell into the trap at once; I think I managed it very well, especially that bit about the idea coming to me in the toilet. It's just such details that help a lot. So the idea came very gently, as if it really was just so that we could both stretch our legs with a walk in town.

He couldn't have said exactly when this fear bit him, when it had fixed its teeth and claws in him, paralysing him. It must have been some time after the visit to the Progress Café, the particular moment that the suspicion gripped him. They'd set a trap for him. Then he realised what this walk in the town meant. It was to give him an 'opportunity' to escape. To wake in him the urge to make that move, thus himself giving Special Branch the evidence, the vital evidence, he hadn't given up to now. Because, certainly, they would have taken the necessary measures to prevent his getting away from them. They would let him make the first move, they'd sweeten him up until he dared. And then they'd reel him in again and hold the trump card they needed. And then there'd be nothing he could do. What could he say? This way he would himself have given them the proof of his guilt, as if he'd signed a declaration that he was guilty. If he made an attempt to get away and they caught him—as they surely would—he would be caught red-handed.

From the moment he began to be afraid that they'd set a trap for him, from the moment that fear ruled his mind, he felt his knees give way. How could he risk doing what he'd decided on yesterday evening when the Chief had said he was going to be transferred to the capital the next morning? Such an attempt might be a double-edged sword. Fine if he succeeded, but if he didn't manage to carry it through the only result would be to give them the weapon they needed against him… from the moment this crack had opened in him, that fear had started to eat away at him or had set an explosive charge within him, from that moment on he didn't have the power to make the split-second decision needed to make his move as soon as an opportunity arose. And there had been many such opportunities during the walk around town, and its extensions. Even right from the barber's, when the Special Branch agent had been stuck in his chair, covered in soap and swathed in towels as he was being shaved; then he'd have been able to make a run for it, he could have risked running for the way out. He'd have taken his chance then, if it hadn't happened that the agent had finished being shaved just then and there was no time left. And then afterwards, on their walk, there'd been chances here and there to escape. It just took nerve. But he hadn't done anything; the fear that this was just what the Special Branch agents wanted had drugged him. And something else occurred to him: maybe there was a third agent following them, ready to spring into action if he made any attempt to get away. No, he hadn't noticed anyone following them, no-one who might be a Special Branch agent. Even so, he'd had the suspicion.

And now, what use was it sitting here in room 717 of the Grand National, with the window closed, pretending to solve the crossword puzzle, trying to think of the river that 'not only drowns but devours'. What was the point in sitting here thinking over all that had happened— and all that hadn't happened—thinking about that unique, unrepeatable chance that the walk in town presented? What was the point? It was much too late now, the chance had passed and wouldn't return, and he hadn't done the slightest thing to exploit it. Much too late! 2.27. In two and a half hours, maybe sooner, the Manager would be knocking at the door. He could no longer do anything, he could no longer think of anything.

Well, our man behaved himself during our walk round the town. No, he made no attempt to escape, which we'd thought would be a possibility. Of course, the fact that he'd behaved like that didn't necessarily mean he was innocent, an innocent man who had nothing to fear. Maybe he'd thought that he wouldn't be able to make it. Maybe he'd discovered that the third man was following us on our walk and that had stopped him. I can't know which of the two it was, or something else, and I'm not interested. The only thing worrying me is what might happen from now on. There's no way I can relax my vigilance. Even now, when I've got him holed up again in room 717 of the Grand National, maybe he'll make a move out of sheer desperation. Jump on me suddenly, hoping to put me out of action... I don't know! I keep on pretending to read the *Evening News*, but all my attention's on the Café Sport man as I watch him struggling with his crossword—and how do I know if his crossword's just camouflage when in fact all this time he's secretly getting ready for the punch he's going to throw at me at any moment?

At the same time I have to admit that I didn't expect him to behave so well during the walk in the town, when if he'd wanted to get away he'd had plenty, or anyway enough, opportunities. How that would have turned out is another matter, since neither I nor the third man were fast asleep. No, there was no possibility that the same thing would happen as had happened with the other Café Sport man. If this one tried to escape, we wouldn't let him be so unlucky—so lucky—as his accomplice. It's right to call him that: his accomplice. Because we wouldn't need any other proof if we had that piece of evidence in our hands, that our man had tried to escape. What stronger proof of guilt could exist than that he'd tried to escape? The other Special Branch agent had been following us all the time. I saw him or felt him near us, ready to go with his pistol in his hand at the vital moment. And me with my own pistol in my hand. And yet nothing happened, and our walk started and finished in total calm. Why? One possibility: that the Café Sport man was innocent and had the calmness and security of the innocent. Even so, innocent people have been arrested by the Special Branch and out of fear of the nightmare of interrogation they were waiting to go through have tried to escape or have killed themselves, simply because they felt they wouldn't be able to stand it. In the case of the Café Sport man, let's allow the possibility that he's innocent, and that's why he didn't make the slightest attempt to escape. Or that he's guilty, but he reckons that they don't have enough evidence to make a case? Or that his accomplice didn't confess to anything, or that if he did confess, he didn't incriminate our man so he has nothing to fear? Or it's not out of the question that there's something I hadn't thought of until now: that he's been informed that his accomplice wasn't taken alive and so he has nothing to worry about. Maybe some other accomplices informed him. I can't know... and I can't know whether there's a person or persons in the Special Branch playing a double game.

As for our walk, it couldn't have gone better. As the basis, the main body of our Plan, and simply as a walk. And I managed the extensions to the walk very neatly, as if they were spur-of-the-moment decisions. And then when I suggested we should talk to each other more informally. The conversations I kept starting—and he, too, started them many times—all those warm and friendly, everyday conversations we had, all we saw, heard, and experienced in the more than four hours of our walk. The shave in the barber's shop, the window-shopping, the little things the two of us stopped to watch, just like the other passers-by, his juice and my iced coffee in the Progress Café, the two girls, the bus trip down to the sea, enjoying ourselves on the beach, the football match with the children's team, the fairground and our little adventure in the House of Mystery, all that, and lots of other things I can't bring to mind right now, all these composed our walk in the town. We shall see if the Plan, the experiment, has succeeded. I shall have to wait. Maybe for a long time, maybe not.

'I'm going crazy in here!' said the Interrogator. 'What the hell can we do to pass the time?'

'Would you like your revenge at chess?'

'Oh, no! I'm fed up with chess. We must think of something.'

'If we had something to read...'

'Bravo! There's an excellent idea. But where can we get a book or a magazine? I'll ask reception. They might not be too pleased to be called after midnight, but never mind. It's a hotel and we can do what we like; we're paying, after all.'

The phone rang six or seven times before reception answered. Finally came a voice that wasn't exactly encouraging—'Who is it?'—like a sentry with his rifle ready and his finger on the trigger saying, 'Who goes there?'

'It's me,' the Interrogator whispered, 'room 717. I know it's rather late to call you, but I wanted to ask if you have any books or magazines... we'd be really grateful.'

'Well, the hotel doesn't have any of its own. But I'll look; maybe in some cupboard there might be some that customers have left behind. I'll send up whatever I find.'

'Great,' said our man as soon as the Interrogator put the phone down. 'We can pass some of the time reading. You know, when I was a boy I read far more than I do now.'

'Oh yes? What sort of thing did you like best?'

'Detective stories. I've read thousands. Well, hundreds.'

The Interrogator frowned. 'Since you're so clued up on detective stories, I'd better take care. Hmm... you might know tricks I'd never imagine.'

The Café Sport man laughed. 'Don't worry! If I knew the sort of tricks you mean, I'd have used them while the two of us were out so long in town, during our walk.'

'Well, I'll tell you what *I* read when I was younger: romances. Knights in armour, heroism, passion, great love affairs...'

'I'd never have thought it.'

'You're always saying "I'd never have thought it." But then, why should you have thought it? We've only just got to know each other.'

In less than five minutes there was a knock at the door; the Interrogator had already unlocked it and was waiting.

'It's not much, but I've brought you the first instalment,' said the employee, probably the one who had answered the phone. 'I'll send up some more in the morning.'

'Don't bother. We just want something for the night, to pass the time.'

'Insomnia, eh? The only cure is to drink a glass of hot milk, straight off, before you go to sleep.'

'Oh yes? I'll try it tomorrow. For tonight, it's too late.'

He carefully double-bolted the door, put the key in his pocket, and left the books—only books, no magazines—on the table.

'What have they fished up?' asked the Café Sport man, who was sitting on the bed and fiddling with his cigarette lighter.

'Four books altogether. I'll read you the titles. First: *A Complete History of the War of 1939–1945.* Second: *A Treasury of Practical Knowledge.* Third: a volume of Chekhov's plays. And last: *The Secrets of the Bedroom.*'

'A broad selection. Take your pick.' He rose from the bed and standing by the window, opened *A Treasury of Practical Knowledge*:

'"Furs: if your fur is a valuable one, it is better to entrust it to a specialist for cleaning and preservation. When your fur coat gets wet, let it dry before brushing with a soft brush."'

'I see you're in a hurry to increase "your practical knowledge", said the Interrogator.

'Why not? Want another one? "Horn. Articles made of animal horn are cleaned with a soft sponge dipped in water and a little ammonia. Then they should be polished with an oiled cloth."'

'For thinning hair... two grams of naphthalene in a bottle of methylated spirit. Mix well. Apply every day.'

The Café Sport man looked at the Interrogator and couldn't understand where he was reading this remedy for thinning hair, 'Look here, *I've* got the *Treasury of Practical Knowledge*, so where did you find that remedy? What *you've* got is Chekhov's plays, isn't it?'

'That's right. It's from *Three Sisters.* In the first act, right at the beginning, we've got Olga, Massa, Irene, Baron Touzebach, Cheboutikin, and Salioni. Cheboutikin, Ivan Romanich Cheboutikin, reads in his newspaper exactly what I've just read.'

Then the Café Sport man went and stood next to the Interrogator, on his right, and bent to look at the book as if he wanted to make sure.

'You found it yourself?'

'Yes.' And on the word 'Yes' he bent down further and turned the page. In the first act, his eye was caught by Versinin's speech to Massa, and as if playing the part of Versinin, he read:

'"*Yes, we shall all be forgotten. Such is our fate, and we can't do anything about it. And all the things that seem serious, important and full of meaning for us now will be forgotten one day—or anyway, they won't seem important any more. It's strange to think that we're utterly unable to tell what will be regarded as great and important in the future and what will be thought of as just paltry and ridiculous. Didn't the discoveries of Copernicus—or of Columbus, if you like—appear useless and unimportant to begin with? Whereas some rubbish written up by an eccentric fool was regarded as a revelation of great truth? It may well be that in time to come the life we live today will seem strange and uncomfortable and stupid and not too clean, either, and perhaps even wicked..."*

"Who can tell? It's just as possible that future genera-tions will think that we lived our lives on a very high plane and remember us with respect. After all, we no longer have tortures and public executions and invasions..."'

He took a sidelong glance at the Interrogator as if in doubt whether to say something. Finally, he made his mind up and spoke:

'I don't imagine you mean that seriously.'

'How do you mean?'

'Well, all that you said about our time and...'

'That was Tuzebach!' the Interrogator interrupted. 'Tuzebach was speaking and I just repeated his point of view.'

'Oh, that's all right then.'

And they carried on reading in turn, more and more warmly and emotionally.

First the Interrogator read:

"*All right then... after we're dead, people will fly about in balloons, the cut of their coats will be different, the sixth sense will be discovered, and possibly even developed and used, for all I know... but I believe life itself will remain the same; it will still be difficult and full of mystery and full of happiness. And in a thousand years' time, people will still be sighing and complaining, 'How hard this business of living is!'—and yet they'll still be scared of death and unwilling to die, just as they are now.*"

"*Well, you know... how shall I put it? I think everything in the world is bound to change gradually—in fact, it's changing before our very eyes. In two or three hundred years, or maybe in a thousand years—it doesn't matter how long exactly—life will be different. It will be happy. Of course, we shan't be able to enjoy that future life, but all the same, what we're living for now is to create it, we work and... yes, we suffer in order to create it. That's the goal of our life, and you might say that's the only happiness we shall ever achieve.*"

"*Man longs for a life like that, and if it isn't here yet, he must imagine it, wait for it, dream about it, prepare for it...*"

"*In the old days, the human race was always making war, its entire existence was taken up with campaigns, advances, retreats, victories... but now all that's out of date.*"

"*How cheerfully and jauntily that band's playing— really I feel as if I wanted to live! Merciful God! The years will pass, and we shall all be gone for good and quite for-gotten... our faces and our voices will be forgotten and people won't even know that there were once three of us here... but our sufferings may mean happiness for the people who come after us... there'll be a time when peace and hap-piness reign in the world, and then we shall be remembered kindly and blessed... the band is playing so cheerfully and joyfully—maybe, if we wait a little longer, we shall find out why we live, why we suffer..."'*

'"What does it matter? Nothing matters!..." Chebu-tikin says. I say that the only thing that matters is how I'm suffering from those sea urchin spines. You know I stood on a sea urchin when we were competing to see who would get to the rock first.'

'But how come we didn't think of the spines be-fore?'

'Oh, the time passed in conversation. The truth is it didn't hurt at the time and I forgot about it, but now they're hurting.'

'I'll call reception,' suggested the Interrogator. 'You shouldn't leave them unattended to. I think I've got a pin, let's see... yes, I've got a couple in my lapel. But we need something else, too.'

As soon as he picked up the phone, the receptionist answered, 'Surely you don't want more books? Have you read them already?'

'No, it's not books we want,' the Interrogator ex-plained. 'We want a little oil, cooking oil. And some cotton wool and... nothing else. What? What happened? One of us stepped on a sea urchin.'

It was another employee who knocked at the door; a young man with eyes swollen with sleep.

'You won't be able to manage it by yourself,' said the Interrogator once the young man had gone and he'd double-bolted the door again.

'You mean you'll perform the operation yourself?'

'Why not? Take off your right shoe and sock.'

'That's what the Chief said to me yesterday evening.'

'Never mind the Chief now. First, I'll light a match to sterilise the pin.'

So he sat on the bed and took off his right shoe and sock.

'You'll see that the spines will come out easily, one by one. Just turn the lamp round so the light doesn't get in my eyes.'

The last hours of night had come. From a certain moment on we were both silent. What more was there to say? We'd talked about everything, and naturally tiredness, lack of sleep, had reduced us to silence.

Sometimes we sat on the chairs and sometimes on the beds, then we'd walk from one wall to the other, or we'd stand in front of the closed window. At some point I began to feel hot and uncomfortable.

'We can't keep the window closed all the time!' I said and opened it.

'I wanted to suggest it myself, but I didn't like to.'

'Why? You should have said. We're stifling with this heat and all this time it never occurred to me to open the window.'

'It's drizzling,' he said, stretching his hand outside.

'Really? So the Manager was right with his weather forecast, and it's starting to rain.'

'Yes, it's really raining now. What's the time? My watch has stopped.'

'Twenty to five.'

'The Manager should arrive any time now.'

'Don't expect him before five. And then we'll be three, just like when we set out.'

We exchanged a few more words about nothing in particular, and then I wanted to go to the toilet. I closed the window and told him to come and stand outside the bathroom door.

'I know the trick! I have to stand there and sing the national anthem, just like the last time.'

It was the force of the sudden draught that did it. With the door and the little window of the toilet open, the wind happened to blow a little more strongly and opened the window in the room. Or maybe it hadn't been properly closed before and the Interrogator hadn't made sure it was closed.

The question was how the draught had slammed the toilet door closed and jammed it. Until that second, all had gone calmly and well, but now the picture changed completely.

When he saw that the window was open and the door of the toilet jammed shut so that the agent couldn't open it, he felt that the draught itself was pulling him. He ran to the window and was out on the ledge with one jump. If he could just manage to get to the fire escape it would be too late for the Interrogator to stop him. The ledge was very narrow and with the greatest care, gluing himself to the wall, he edged along. He wasn't thinking of anything at that moment; he was incapable of thought and anyway there was no need. He simply grasped the instinct that had woken in him: to get away!

As for the Interrogator, the moment the toilet door closed and he could hear nothing, he felt like a rat in a trap. He pulled at the door but realised it was jammed. He pulled again: nothing. Then he threw himself against it with all his weight, and it gave way.

'You can't get away!' he shouted as he ran into the room with his pistol in his hand.

But he didn't see him there. He must have managed to get out of the window and onto the ledge. The light in the room—the overhead light and the two bedside lamps—stopped him from seeing outside. Within seconds, he turned out all the lights. The Café Sport man was out there on the ledge, three or four metres from the window, clinging to the wall and inching along. He could see him clearly now that the lights were out. The rain was stronger now and stopped the Café Sport man from getting along more quickly.

'You can't get away, you hear?' he shouted for a second time as he leant on the windowsill and took aim.

Then the Café Sport man stopped and half turned towards the window. His heart was in his mouth. The game was up. His last-minute attempt to escape wasn't going to succeed. Just a little more, another two seconds, if the toilet door had just stayed jammed two seconds more. Two seconds more and he'd have been able to jump onto the fire escape, run down it like lightning and get into the street, then disappear somewhere in the direction of the station, somewhere among the empty carriages or wherever luck and instinct led him. Just so long as he could get in touch with the organisation. But now it was too late, the agent was standing at the window, three metres away, the pistol aimed at him, its two barrels—two little circles. Two little circles in front of him again, ready to bite him, not for him to bite them. To bite him with two little round deadly teeth. How to get away from those two little circles that were watching him like two hypnotic eyes, three metres away, fixing him to the ledge, nailing him to the wall. Below was chaos. Seven long storeys between him and the ground.

'It's too late now!' I called to him, but not so loudly as to wake up the whole Grand National.

I didn't want a huge disturbance, that would only make difficulties. I took a quick look and saw that the time was about ten to five. If the Manager arrived now, he could run round to the fire escape to cut him off, or he could get to it from the window of another room. Or he and the hotel people would open a safety net below. Yes, if the Manager came, for sure the two of us would be able to put everything right again.

Like an acrobat on the twenty-five centimetres of the ledge, swaying on a rope stretched seven floors up, he didn't know what to do. To carry on towards the fire escape would be pointless. The agent wouldn't dare follow him, but he'd shoot. And there was no chance that crack shot would miss. With the lights out in the room, and himself lit by the spill of light from the floodlights in the station yard he was an easy target. He'd thrown away the unique chance of the walk in town, and he'd left to the last minute the leap he should have dared to make much earlier, when there were greater chances of success.

'You can't get away, you hear?' came the voice of the Interrogator out of the abyss-like darkness, reaching him there where he was stuck to the wall and waiting.

What was he waiting for? To carry on to the fire escape meant a pistol shot. And the agent could aim wherever he chose, such as his legs, simply to wound him. But then he wouldn't be able to stand still on a twenty-five centimetre ledge. He would collapse, clawing harder still and helplessly at the wall, but how could he hang on? And he'd fall into the emptiness below him. Seven storeys separated him from the flagstones of the court-yard. With his attempt to escape he'd given them the proof they wanted and had been perhaps trying to pro-voke. As if he'd told them, or written down, 'I'm guilty.' So, what could he do? Go back to the room? After such a confession of guilt? They'd have him under their thumbs, knowing he was guilty and the only thing they'd try to do was to find out more, everything, about the organisation. The interrogation they'd subject him to at Central would be nothing like the interrogation at Special Branch back in the town. No, there was a third possibility: to let himself slide down into the emptiness from seven floors up. But he didn't have the courage to go voluntarily to his death. He knew, there and then, that he couldn't do it.

It was a good thing the Chief had chosen a room that wasn't on the ground floor. If it had been on the ground floor, then with the bad luck of the toilet door jamming, and me being separated from our man for a few seconds, it would have been too late to catch him. He'd have jumped into the street, and how could I follow him in the darkness? But now, yes, he'd managed to slip out onto the ledge from the open window, and I'd got him stuck there, three metres away, and I could reason with him and get him back into my hands. Not that it wouldn't be horribly difficult to get him back into the room. He could miss his step and we'd lose him. Or he could deliberately jump. The fourth man in Operation Toilet Paper had taken cyanide. The suspect—or rather, now proven, the guilty man—from the Café Sport might leap to his death. I mustn't hurry. I must take the greatest care to avoid that catastrophe: the suspect was no longer just a suspect but guilty. I know that he's guilty. The Plan yielded its result, the famous Plan worked in him and gave us the proof we didn't have, his confession, which we can't know if we would have got otherwise. I must be careful. Anyway, the Manager will turn up at any moment. The door's locked, but when he comes he'll understand what's happened, he'll guess and he'll open the door; he'll find another key or he'll force his way in, or he'll shoot off the lock. There's no problem there. The only thing is not to move away from the window, not to take my eyes off him even for a second, so that I can get him back beside me.

But finally fear overcame him. The fear that if he fell into their hands again, if the Special Branch got him once more, he wouldn't be able to stand what awaited him. No, he wasn't going to do them the favour of going back to them marked with the confession of guilt he'd himself given them. He saw the abyss below him. His agony would be over within a second if he just put his foot over the ledge. Twenty-five centimetres was nothing. But he just didn't have the power to take that step to his death. At the station, an engine had started shunting. Was it just the engine? Were there carriages, too? He couldn't tell in the darkness. He could see the two lights of the engine moving like two little circles, two little circles fixed on him. That's what he was thinking of at that moment: her breasts, all of her. 'At the post office?' 'Why not?' 'OK, seven o'clock at the post office, in front of the Foreign Registered counter.' He covered his eyes with his hand so as to no longer see the engine's lights, the two little circles of her breasts which they were presenting to him, to his heart. But there was no hope. Whatever was going to happen, let it happen quickly, now! He'd provoke the Interrogator, infuriate him, make him lose his calm and shoot him. Then he'd sink into the abyss that was waiting for him, altogether sink into it, with a bullet in his side or in his guts, and it would be simple and inevitable. Everything would be over right here, in the courtyard of the Grand National.

'Move towards the window; don't play the acrobat. I know you're guilty, you're not the "peace-loving citizen" you said you were. You yourself have shown us that you're guilty, you've confessed your guilt. So, move back towards the window!' I say to him, and I look him straight in the eyes.

An alarm clock shrills in some room of the Grand National; someone who'd left his window open onto the courtyard and was getting up early to go to work, or perhaps one of the hotel employees starting his shift.

'Don't stare at me like that, you heard the alarm clock. Come now while it's still quiet and we won't turn the hotel upside down. Don't make me use more drastic methods, like shooting you in the legs or somewhere; you realise you wouldn't be able to stay on the ledge. You'd slip off it and below you is emptiness; you wouldn't survive if you slipped off. Come back, slowly and gently.'

He doesn't react to what I say; he looks at me with the same distant gaze, as if looking not in fact at me but at someone else, or something beyond me, something far away on the horizon, a non-existent horizon: beyond me there's just the wall with the door of room 717. In a little while the Manager will knock, and then the two of us, the Manager and I, will have him cornered there where he clambered onto the ledge, and it would be a pathetic end for our prisoner who dared to try to escape. I've got my gaze fixed on him; I'm standing at the window with my pistol in my hand. I lean out a little and say to him:

'Tigris.'

I said the word 'Tigris', just like that, as it suddenly came to me.

'Tigris,' I said again, and he looked at me with an even more deeply lost gaze.

Then I said to him:

'Tigris is that mysterious river we were both looking for, for such a long time, four down, the river that "not only drowns but devours". There, just now it came to me. We found it at last!'

And at the same time as I'm explaining four down, the same time as I repeat 'Tigris', something collapses inside me, I feel I'm sinking or being washed away, that little word 'Tigris' which I said in all innocence without thinking of any consequence it might have, that word is tied up with the whole Plan I'm responsible for carrying out, it's tied up with the whole charade I've been playing. The word 'Tigris' is the end of a ball of string I was pulling, and the ball is unwinding, it's like the end of the scarf the conjuror pulls and out come scarf after scarf, one tied to the next, a whole string of multi-coloured scarves, as soon as I said 'Tigris' it was as if a different light shone on every little thing he and I have gone through since seven this morning when we set out from the courtyard of Special Branch, I can't hand him over, no, I just can't, if he hadn't climbed out of the window and perched on the ledge, if he hadn't at the last moment made that jump and confession in one, if I hadn't felt he was guilty, if everything had only gone on normally until the moment the draught came and jammed the toilet door, then maybe this crack wouldn't have opened in me, but now I know he's guilty, he himself has given me the proof of his guilt, it was I who managed to break him so that he gave us what we didn't have and perhaps wouldn't have been able to get until the end, the confession of his guilt, the charade I played for so long had its result, I can't hand him over, his very confession stops me, it was I who made him confess, it was I who pretended to have feelings, that I felt friendly towards him, that I was a man with a heart, I who put on a human face, played the part of a human being, but now I've discovered that I wasn't just playing the part of a human being, I've discovered that there is after all something human in me, I can't hand him over, I see him standing opposite me and it's as if we're still carrying on our walk through the town, the Plan worked like clockwork, I made every effort for the Plan to succeed, that perfect Plan, I can't hand him over, the two of us are friends, the pair of us are friends now, another alarm clock goes off and breaks the silence of the Grand National, two or three windows light up on the sixth floor and on the fourth, the Manager will knock on the door at any moment, I can't hand him over, it's impossible for me to hand him over, one by one pictures from our walk in the town flash before me, the shave at the barber's, the first part of the stroll, the shop windows we gazed into, the accident we witnessed among the other onlookers, the Progress Café, the two girls, the trip to the beach, the stones we skipped on the sea to see who could make them bounce farthest, the fairground, the House of Mystery, the return to the Grand National, the cooking oil cotton wool and pin and me bending down to take out the spines one by one, the crossword, four down, 'Tigris' is the river that 'not only drown but devours,' no, I can't hand him over.

'Go!' I say to him and I look him straight in the eye.

He doesn't say anything; he doesn't try to go.

'Go!' I say, and wave him away with my pistol.

He keeps on staring at me.

'Go!' I say for the third time. He doesn't move, he's motionless. The Manager will appear, wherever he is.

'Go!' I say to him.

The Plan worked perfectly, except that it turned round and bit me back; the Plan is the scorpion that stings itself to death.

'Go!' I say to him.

I bend down and aim at him, a train whistles hoarsely, coming or going, the rain keeps falling, I see him in the rain, I see him dissolving in the rain, no, he's not dissolving, he's there on the ledge.

'Go! Go now, or I'll shoot!' I order him, I beg him.

We've got no more time, there, the Manager's already knocking at the door, knocking and knocking, but I don't open the door.

'Go!'

He doesn't take any notice, the rain's tipping down on him, I can't hand him over, the Manager's knocking more and more loudly, he's throwing himself against the door, the door stands up to it.

'Go!'

The Manager shoots the lock, the door springs open, the Manager comes into the room, stands on the threshold for a second, pistol in hand.

'Go!'

I can't hand him over, the Plan, the perfect Plan, is like a perfect crime that isn't perfect, we foresaw everything down to the last detail, we worked it all out with mathematical precision, we'd made a masterpiece, but there was a flaw, a flaw and I can't at this moment think any further than that, the Manager fixes me with his eyes, he can't believe what he sees, what he hears, the Special Branch Interrogator, the man so faithful to the Regime, the fanatic for the Regime, me, I'm saying to our prisoner, 'Go!' and I'm trying to get him to escape, the Manager of course has no idea what's happening inside me, the Regime is no longer the first thing on my mind, in my heart, the man on the ledge comes first, the man on the ledge and I are a pair, are friends, a walk together in town, walking together in life, one tied to the other with something we in the Special Branch hadn't bargained for, there's a flaw in the Plan, there's a flaw in the Regime, no, people aren't divided into those who are with the Regime and those who aren't, a flaw, a critical flaw, the Regime is perforated by just such a flaw, a flaw that will blow us up into the air like dynamite. I can't hand him over, I'm in a position to know what's waiting for me, but I won't hand him over, I won't hand over that other human being who is looking at me from three metres away, clinging to the ledge, clinging on to me, a flaw is spreading illicitly into everything we thought certain and secure, there's a flaw somewhere here around us inside us, a flaw.

'Go!'

He sees the Manager aiming his pistol at the agent, he sees the Manager coming from the door towards the agent, threatening but also doubtful, his eyes and his pistol fixed on the agent, he sees the agent at once turn his pistol to aim at the Manager, ready to shoot him and stop him from getting to the window, but also turning to look at him out there on the ledge and to say, one more time, 'Go!' And now he sees the Manager, as if at last now sure of what was going on, shoot the agent in his right hand so that his pistol falls to the floor, blood spurts, and only now, as the agent doubles up and staggers, only now does he realise that the 'Go!' he'd kept saying to him wasn't a trick, wasn't a trap, only now does he feel that that 'Go!' was real, and only now does he feel an instinct to run to the agent, to take him in his arms, to stand by him as a friend, he takes a step along the ledge towards the window, he takes another step, the Manager is standing there with both of them in front of his pistol barrel, the rain keeps falling, the ledge is slippery, he tries to cling to the wall but the ledge is slippery, he slips, and he just manages to see the courtyard coming up to him, the courtyard with its big square flagstones like the across and down of a crossword.

MODERN
GREEK
CLASSICS

C.P. CAVAFY
Selected Poems
Translated by David Connolly

Cavafy is by far the most translated and well-known Greek poet internationally. Whether his subject matter is historical, philosophical or sensual, Cavafy's unique poetic voice is always recognizable by its ironical, suave, witty and world-weary tones.

ODYSSEUS ELYTIS
1979 NOBEL PRIZE FOR LITERATURE
In the Name of Luminosity and Transparency
With an Introduction by Dimitris Daskalopoulos

The poetry of Odysseus Elytis owes as much to the ancients and Byzantium as to the surrealists of the 1930s and the architecture of the Cyclades, bringing romantic modernism and structural experimentation to Greece. Collected here are the two speeches Elytis gave on his acceptance of the 1979 Nobel Prize for Literature.

M. KARAGATSIS
The Great Chimera
Translated by Patricia Barbeito

A psychological portrait of a young French woman, Marina, who marries a sailor and moves to the island of Syros, where she lives with her mother-in-law and becomes acquainted with the Greek way of life. Her fate grows entwined with that of the boats and when economic downturn arrives, it brings passion, life and death in its wake.

ANDREAS LASKARATOS
Reflections
Translated by Simon Darragh
With an Introduction by Yorgos Y. Alisandratos

Andreas Laskaratos was a writer and poet, a social thinker and, in many ways, a controversialist. His *Reflections* sets out, in a series of calm, clear and pithy aphorisms, his uncompromising and finely reasoned beliefs on morality, justice, personal conduct, power, tradition, religion and government.

ALEXANDROS PAPADIAMANDIS
Fey Folk
Translated by David Connolly

Alexandros Papadiamandis holds a special place in the history of Modern Greek letters, but also in the heart of the ordinary reader. *Fey Folk* follows the humble lives of quaint, simple-hearted folk living in accordance with centuries-old traditions and customs, described here with both reverence and humour.

ALEXANDROS RANGAVIS
The Notary
Translated by Simon Darragh

A mystery set on the island of Cephalonia on the eve of the Greek Revolution of 1821, this classic work of Rangavis is an iconic tale of suspense and intrigue, love and murder. *The Notary* is Modern Greek literature's contribution to the tradition of early crime fiction, alongside E.T.A. Hoffman, Edgar Allan Poe and Wilkie Collins.

GEORGE SEFERIS

1963 NOBEL PRIZE FOR LITERATURE

Novel and Other Poems

Translated by Roderick Beaton

Often compared during his lifetime to T.S. Eliot, George Seferis is noted for his spare, laconic, dense and allusive verse in the Modernist idiom of the first half of the twentieth century. Seferis better than any other writer expresses the dilemma experienced by his countrymen then and now: how to be at once Greek and modern.

MAKIS TSITAS

As God is My Witness

Translated by Joshua Barley

A hilariously funny and achingly sad portrait of Greek society during the crisis years, as told by a lovable anti-hero. Fifty-year-old Chrysovalantis, who has recently lost his job and struggles with declining health, sets out to tell the story of his life, roaming the streets of Athens on Christmas Eve with nothing but a suitcase in hand.

ILIAS VENEZIS

Serenity

Translated by Joshua Barley

Inspired by the author's own experience of migration, the novel follows the journey of a group of Greek refugees from Asia Minor who settle in a village near Athens. It details the hatred of war, the love of nature that surrounds them, the hostility of their new neighbours and eventually their adaptation to a new life.

GEORGIOS VIZYENOS
Thracian Tales
Translated by Peter Mackridge

These short stories bring to life Vizyenos' native Thrace, a corner of Europe where Greece, Turkey and Bulgaria meet. Through masterful psychological portayals, each story keeps the reader in suspense to the very end: Where did Yorgis' grandfather travel on his only journey? What was Yorgis' mother's sin? Who was responsible for his brother's murder?

GEORGIOS VIZYENOS
Moskov Selim
Translated by Peter Mackridge

A novella by Georgios Vizyenos, one of Greece's best-loved writers, set in Thrace during the time of the Russo-Turkish War, whose outcome would decide the future of southeastern Europe. *Moskov Selim* is a moving tale of kinship, despite the gulf of nationality and religion.

NIKIFOROS VRETTAKOS
Selected Poems
Translated by David Connolly

The poems of Vrettakos are firmly rooted in the Greek landscape and coloured by the Greek light, yet their themes and sentiment are ecumenical. His poetry offers a vision of the paradise that the world could be, but it is also imbued with a deep and painful awareness of the dark abyss that the world threatens to become.

AN ANTHOLOGY
Rebetika: Songs from
the Old Greek Underworld
Edited and translated by Katharine Butterworth & Sara Schneider

The songs in this book are a sampling of the urban folk songs of Greece during the first half of the twentieth century. Often compared to American blues, rebetika songs are the creative expression of the *rebetes*, people living a marginal and often underworld existence on the fringes of established society.

·15,50